'Gripping. I raced through it'

A.M. Howell, author of *The Garden of Lost Secrets*

'A beautifully rendered adventure. You'll

cheer for its brave, big-hearted hero'

Carlie Sorosiak, author of *I Cosmo*

'Compelling, moving, illuminating . . .'

Mike Leigh

'An enchanting tapestry of beauty and bravery'

Emma Read, author of *Milton the Mighty*

'Art's journey into the wicked heart of the witch

trials is immersive, and vividly drawn'

Hannah Tooke, author of *The Unadoptables*

The FOREST of MOON and SWORD

The FOREST of MOON and SWORD

AMY RAPHAEL

Orion

ORION CHILDREN'S BOOKS
First published in Great Britain in 2021 by Hodder and Stoughton

1 3 5 7 9 10 8 6 4 2

A CIP catalogue record for this book
is available from the British Library.

ISBN 978 1 510 10835 6
Waterstones Signed Edition 978 1 510 10965 0

Printed and bound in Great Britain by Clays Ltd, Elcograph S.p.A.

The paper and board used in this book are made
from wood from responsible sources.

Orion Children's Books
An imprint of
Hachette Children's Group
Part of Hodder and Stoughton
Carmelite House
50 Victoria Embankment
London EC4Y 0DZ

An Hachette UK Company
www.hachette.co.uk
www.hachettechildrens.co.uk

For Bonnie, always

"I took a deep breath and listened to the old brag of my heart. I am, I am, I am."

Sylvia Plath, *The Bell Jar*

1

12 June 1647

I wake up in the dark.

I remember.

They are coming.

They will be here soon.

Word came this afternoon from the next village that the soldiers had crossed the border from England into Scotland, their weary horses hauling empty carts.

The wall is cold against my back. My body is stiff. I slowly stretch out my legs and the floorboard beneath me creaks.

'Art! Keep still,' whispers Mother.

We sit, my mother and I, in heavy silence.

I am suddenly glad of the dark because I can no longer see the desperation in her eyes.

'Hold my hand,' I say, so quietly that I don't expect her to respond. I place my hand on the dusty attic floor and she strokes it, her fingers as light and cold as the first snow, then wraps it in her hand and squeezes it tight.

I can barely hear the shallow breath of the women sitting on the other side of the attic. I have never met them before. They turned up at our house late this afternoon and told Mother they were scared their husbands might hand them over to the soldiers. Mother took them in and told them that as long they couldn't be seen or heard, they wouldn't be discovered. They are strangers, but I desperately want them to be safe.

I shut my eyes tight and try to imagine what I would be doing on an ordinary day. Perhaps Mother would be setting the fire against the last chill of spring while I read the Bible out loud to her. I would be hungry, as always. Oh, how hungry I am now, how thirsty. I try to stay still, but I need to use the chamber pot so badly.

I cannot leave the attic. Mother says hiding here is our best chance of evading capture. By the time the news of the soldiers came, it was too late to run. All we can do is wait. And hope against hope.

I huddle as close to Mother as possible, and she puts her mouth right up against my ear, so close that it tickles.

'Are you sure you know how to find the trapdoor in the dark?'

'Yes, Mother. And I am sure I will be able to fit through it. We have practised enough times.' I immediately feel guilty for the edge in my voice, but I can't take it back.

We sit in silence before Mother speaks softly again. I know this story well. This is the story she tells to settle me when I have a fever, but this time I sense that I need to calm her too, so I squeeze her hand even tighter. 'When you were seven, I came home one afternoon to find you gone. I looked everywhere. I was beside myself. Eventually, as night was falling, I asked some townspeople to help search for you in the forest.' Her voice is unsteady. 'I thought you had been taken.'

It soothes me to remember that summer's morning, the mist burning off the fields and the sun already warm

16

on my skin. I had seen a cloth sack on a neighbour's doorstep that was tied lightly at the top and that somehow seemed to be moving. Inside, I found four tiny kittens, three ginger and one pure black, all tiny and helpless, their mouths making silent mews as they blinked up at me. As I peered into the sack, the black kitten climbed above the others and pressed its face against mine. My heart soared. How I had longed for a black cat! Then my heart sank. At the bottom of the bag were three large stones, to weigh the sack down.

How could anybody plan to throw the sack in the river and drown these tiny, helpless kittens?

I removed the stones, threw them to the ground and ran, feeling the warmth of the kittens as I clutched the twitching sack to my chest.

I don't know how long I ran through the forest, but eventually I stopped by a small pond and set the sack down. The kittens looked up at me with their round, bright eyes, and a wave of pure love washed over me. I had saved them!

'When we finally found you by the pond, you were asleep and rigid with cold. The kittens you had tried so desperately to save had run away.' Mother sighs. 'All but one. Malkin was stretched out next to you, her black paws resting on your arm.'

Malkin. As black as night and as devoted to me as I was to her.

'I was furious,' says Mother, gently stroking my long, curly hair. 'I wanted to shake you to make you understand how much you'd scared me.'

Mother's face was drained of colour when she found Malkin and me. I looked up and saw her long red hair, as straight as an arrow, her face paler even than usual and flooded with concern, her green eyes brimming with tears. I had saved the kittens, but Mother had saved me. She always does.

She wrapped me in a woollen blanket and held me close, her heart beating furiously through her thin summer dress.

'I am so sorry about Malkin.' She squeezes my hand and continues. 'I know how much you loved her. You thought you'd never get over her death, but you are stronger than you think, Art Flynt.'

My beloved Malkin. Slaughtered less than a year ago by an unknown neighbour for being a so-called witch's cat. We mummified her body and laid her to rest inside the wall above the door, to ward off evil forces. I don't know why Mother doesn't think Malkin can help us now.

The attic is getting colder as the night deepens. I bring my legs up to my chest and rest my chin on my knees.

We sit in silence again.

A loud bang makes me jump. I stiffen.

'It's the wind playing with the stable door, Mother,' I whisper.

Mother's body is frozen with fear.

Another bang, this time louder and closer. The heavy wood of the front door being flung open.

Then – nothing.

The wind again. It must be the wind. Please let it be so.

I know Mother shut the front door carefully. I know it is not the wind.

'Search every room!' The voice booms through the house, as though the walls are made of paper and not thick, thick stone.

Mother's breath is warm in my ear. 'Aunt Elizabeth will care for you. She is a strange sister, but I do believe that she will take you in with open arms. I love you, Art. Always. Carry me in your heart.' She puts her hand in her pocket and gives me something in the dark. 'Take this letter and read it only when it is safe to do so.'

I put it carefully in my pocket and open my mouth, but no words come. The footsteps on the wooden stairs are heavy and deliberate.

'Go, my child. Go now.'

'But, Mother …'

I don't move. I cannot say goodbye, not now, not like this. The footsteps are in the bedroom below. A man laughs as though this is some kind of game. I hear a chair being dragged along the floor, out of my bedroom and into the hallway. One of the soldiers pushes at the attic door. It always catches. Before, it made me cross. Now, it gives me time.

I jump to my feet. I locate the trapdoor above my head.

Push the small square of wood aside. Pull myself up into the apex of the house. I have practised this so many times in the past few weeks, but always with Mother telling me what to do and praising my agility.

I can hear the attic door below being lifted up.

I push the trapdoor back in place and crouch on top of it.

'Traitors! Witches! *Scottish* witches! You will burn in hell.' The soldier's voice is ablaze with pure hatred.

My mouth is dry. I cannot swallow. My legs shake uncontrollably. I shut my eyes and count slowly, as Mother told me to.

100. 99. 98. 97. 96. 95.

One of the women emits a high-pitched wail as she is lowered through the attic door.

'Silence, woman! Silence, all of you!'

The soldier's tone is so sharp that the woman falls silent. All I can hear is muffled voices as the soldiers direct Mother and the women out of the attic and down the stairs.

50. 49. 48.

The front door slams.

Now I am alone.

10. 9. 8.

My legs are shaking hard. I can no longer feel my feet.

3. 2. 1.

I breathe in and out slowly before standing up. The space is narrow but tall, with a small window on one side. I look out across the fields, biting my nails. The moon is bright and the puddles on the track leading away from the farm are finally starting to dry up after weeks of rain. If I balance on the old milking stool, I can just about see the four soldiers and their horses and carts. The horses stand patiently, occasionally flicking their tails, unaware of what is happening around them. I long to put my arms around my own horse's neck, but Lady will have to wait.

One of the soldiers lines up the women. I can see the first three women, but the remaining three, including Mother, are just out of sight.

I strain to hear. 'Do what I say and no one will be hurt,' says the chief soldier. He stands with his legs apart, one hand thrust deep in his pocket and the other pulling at his huge beard as though it is some kind of prize. He is as vain as Uncle Samuel, who used to admire himself in the polished stone every Sunday morning before church.

The women stare at the ground.

The chief soldier reaches into the cart closest to him and throws a coil of coarse rope at another soldier.

'Hastings, tie them up.'

'Yes, sir.'

Whoever Hastings is takes a knife from his belt and starts cutting the rope.

'Five of you will be executed at dawn,' says the chief soldier. 'There will be a short trial first. We know you are all guilty of being witches, of course, so think of the trial as a mere formality. One of you will be taken straight to England.'

Who? Who will be saved? The thought that it might not be Mother chills my blood.

Hastings stands behind the woman at the start of the line and wrenches her hands behind her back. He wraps the rope around her wrists three times, pulling it until she flinches. He walks methodically along the line tying up each of the women's wrists.

'Throw them in the cart,' says the chief soldier.

Hastings pushes one woman into the cart as though

she is an animal. He pushes another. A third.

Mother must be standing with the other two women, but I cannot see her.

I stand on tiptoes on the stool. As it sways, I grab hold of the window ledge. The stool falls and I tumble to the floor. Fool! *What if they heard me?*

As I jump to my feet and step back on to the stool, the chief soldier below laughs so hard that I think he must have lost his reason. But at least he doesn't look up. He doesn't know I'm here.

Clouds obscure the moon. I wipe away some of the dirt on the window with my sleeve, though still I see only darkness. I allow myself a moment to remember all those times my best friend Cecily and I used to hang out of the attic window and blow at the clouds until they drifted away from the sun, laughing so hard when the sun reappeared that our stomachs hurt.

'Please,' I whisper, squeezing my eyes shut. 'Please

let me see Mother one last time.'

When I open my eyes, the clouds have vanished and the moon is bright.

Malkin is helping me!

The soldiers are guiding the horses and carts down the dirt track. The wheels bump in and out of puddles. One of the soldiers leans to the side and spits into the earth. Leaving a marker behind and taking Mother away. Taking away everything I have.

Five women huddle together in the first cart, their faces hidden. I stare and stare at the solitary woman in the second cart, at the woman who is to be taken to England, to a fate unknown.

As the second cart turns a bend, I see the woman glance up at the attic window.

I see Mother.

2

All I want to do is sit on this wobbly stool and think of Mother. She said I could read the letter only when it was safe to do so. Here, alone in the secret room at the top of the house I love so much, with the moon blazing bright, is as safe as I can imagine. I take the letter out of my pocket, unfold it carefully and hold it up to the moonlight.

A deep breath.

My beloved Art,

I write this in haste. If you have this letter in your hands, it is because the soldiers have taken me. As you know, Kelso has been sending men to battle since war broke out five years ago, but we have yet to experience bloodshed on our doorstep. England, however, is broken in two. It is being destroyed by civil war between those who are for the king and those who are for parliament. People on both sides are uncertain of what the future holds. They are scared. As always in times of great fear, there are scapegoats. Women are sacrificed.

I am hoping that the soldiers take me all the way to Essex, in the south-east of England. This is where, in the parish of Manningtree, witch trials have been scheduled on the summer solstice, the longest day of the year. They say that as many as a hundred women will be murdered that day. But the trials must be stopped!

The thought of never seeing you again is unbearable and I shall do everything in my power to survive. Whatever happens, I will not go gently.

I take a moment to steady my hand, which shakes uncontrollably.

I have some advice for you. You may not need it, but I am your mother and I want to make your life less painful in any way I can. Your journey will ebb and flow, like a river searching for the sea. You will not, I know, be dragged under. Like any journey, it will begin with the first step.

You will meet your guides along the way – be open to them.

Be on your guard, but do not be afraid to take risks. Let love give you courage.

Always believe in your destiny.

My love for you is infinite. My heart is with you always.

God bless you, my child.

Mother

P.S. You will find my recipe book in the drawer beneath the kitchen sink. Let only those you trust with your life see it. Others will regard it with scorn, as a book of magic.

The book of magic! When the war started, Father threatened to burn Mother's recipe book, declaring that it would stop men and women lining up outside our house, asking to be saved. Thomas and I sat at the top of the stairs late one night, holding hands and listening to Mother and Father argue. The calmer Mother remained, the more impatience we could hear in Father's voice. The kitchen door was ajar and words floated up the stairs. I only remember three, repeated again and again by Father: *Potions. Poison. Witch.*

But I know the truth. It is an honour to be trusted with Mother's recipe book. Helping people to heal isn't about magic, it's about compassion.

*

I promised Mother that I would go straight to Aunt Elizabeth's house, but I decide to wait until tomorrow. It's not as though she will notice my absence – she doesn't yet know that Mother has been taken. Besides, the idea of living with Aunt is loathsome. It's hard to believe that she is Mother's sister. She is as cold as a winter burn, her hands are bony and her brown eyes indifferent. Mother, meanwhile, was – *is* – as warm as the midsummer sun, wise and loving, her mouth quick to smile, her green eyes bright, her hair the warm copper colour of leaves in autumn. When Ann and Patrick Percy and their twin babies moved to our small town of Kelso, Aunt decided immediately that she disliked the *idea* of them simply because they weren't born here. Mother argued with her. *Always be kind*, she said. She took remedies to their house on the edge of the town when the twins were poorly, which Aunt considered madness. *Who knows what you might catch in a house full of diseased strangers?*

But I don't want to think about Aunt. I fold the letter up and cry so hard that I cannot catch my breath.

When there are no more tears left, I leave the attic, walk straight past Mother's room without looking and go to the stable. Lady nuzzles me when I put my arms tightly around her neck, as though she knows my heart is broken. I am suddenly so tired that I can barely stand and I curl up in the corner of her stable, barely noticing the sharp straw and instead listening to Lady's slow, calm breathing until I fall into a deep, dreamless sleep.

3

13 June 1647

Eight days to summer solstice

The pew is hard and uncomfortable and I have to force myself to sit still. Sun streams into the church through the stained-glass windows, but here, at the very back, little light ever falls and the air holds a chill even on warm days. I wrap my woollen blanket around my shoulders, but I can't stop shivering. Out of the corner of my eye I can see my cousins Arthur, Dorothy and Anne sitting next to Aunt Elizabeth, unable to stop twitching when they should be sitting still. Aunt sits primly at the far end of the pew, close to the aisle, her mouth set in a thin, mean line.

Neither of us looks at one another. She has not uttered a word to me since I walked into the church and it's not because I was a minute or two late. My mother and I have clearly brought shame on the family. I feel utterly alone.

The church falls silent as the minister, a short man with thinning hair and a sagging stomach, climbs into his pulpit. He bangs his Bible down on the lectern and peers out into the congregation. He looks at each row of packed pews, running his hand through tufts of hair and pulling at his beaky red nose. I interlace my fingers and stare at my bitten nails. When I look up, he is glaring at me, his face pinched.

'People of Kelso and any visitors from local border towns, I welcome you,' says the minister, holding his arms open. He pauses as though waiting for applause, but none comes. He is worse than Hastings and Uncle Samuel put together, I think to myself.

He takes the Bible from the lectern and holds it in

both hands. 'You may have heard – in fact, I am sure you have heard – that English soldiers came last night to round up more witches. They took half a dozen women from this town alone.'

He suddenly thrusts the Bible in the air. 'People! The devil is among us. Scotland is no longer safe! There are witches, witches, witches everywhere! You have the right to know the truth: Agnes Flynt was harbouring witches in this very town and putting all our lives in danger.'

Do not mention my mother! I am almost on my feet when I see Aunt Elizabeth frowning and shaking her head at me. Anger surges through my body but I stay seated.

'Agnes Flynt not only let known witches into her house, but she also treated them as though they were mere *women*.' Spittle flies from the minister's mouth.

'We all know the truth. Agnes Flynt made potions! I could list at least thirteen men who drank her potions in good faith when the measles and smallpox were upon us, and died shortly afterwards.'

Lies. All lies.

Those men were almost dead when Mother gave them the so-called potions! Their wives had come to our house and begged her for remedies. How dare he blame her for everything that has gone wrong in the town; perhaps he is envious of her because people preferred to share their troubles with her instead of him.

'There is more,' says the minister triumphantly. 'Agnes Flynt has a third nipple! She has a birthmark on her back. I am telling you all: her body is decorated with the marks of the devil.'

The congregation gasps. People in the pews in front turn to stare at me and, feeling my cheeks blazing red, I lower my head. I am not ashamed of my mother, but I want to run out of the church, through the graveyard, across the green and home. I want to take Lady into the forest and feel the trees close ranks behind me, like my own private army.

I glance to the end of the pew, where Aunt Elizabeth's angular frame blocks my exit. I am stronger than I think. That's what Mother said. If I keep telling myself, it has to become true. I straighten my back, put my hands in my lap and look beyond the minister to the giant silver pipes of the organ, lined up like a row of oversized swords. The townspeople turn their attention back to the minister.

'We have done what we can to protect ourselves. We carved intertwining circles on to our doors to defend our houses from evil. We have to be more vigilant.' He pauses to wipe more spittle from his mouth. 'Many of us survived measles, typhus, scurvy and tuberculosis, and even the plague. As a small community, we have only sent a dozen young men to war. We are fortunate. King James freed us from hundreds of witches and now that mantle has been taken over by Matthew Hopkins, the Witchfinder General.'

I shiver as he waves the Bible wildly in the air. 'Indeed,

41

the great Matthew Hopkins is our friend. A man I have never met, but about whom I hear great, great things. A man who resides in the south-east of England, but whose soldiers work tirelessly here on the borders of Scotland and England to rid us of women. Of course, I don't mean *all* women, just the ones who are witches. Hopkins has dedicated his life to killing witches. Kill witches!'

Who is this Hopkins, this Witchfinder, the man who took my mother from me?

Cousin Arthur's knees are twitching furiously. His mother smacks his legs and he sits perfectly still, his eyes tightly shut.

The people at the front of the church start chanting. 'Kill all witches! Kill all witches!'

Aunt Elizabeth pulls her children closer to her. She raises her right hand and touches her forehead with the tips of her fingers. She touches the centre of her chest, her left shoulder and then her right. The sign of the cross.

She looks straight at me and says, 'Amen.'

I stand up, pull my woollen blanket tightly around my shoulders, push past Aunt Elizabeth and my cousins and rush into the graveyard, where I lean against the ancient oak, trying to catch my breath. Thoughts swirl around my mind like a sudden breeze picking up autumn leaves and making them dance wildly.

'I saw you rush out of the church. Coward.'

Jack Norman leans on a gravestone in front of me. Two more boys and three girls stand behind him. I only recognise Cecily.

'Why weren't you forced to sit on the Stool of Repentance, Flynt?' asks Jack, his blue eyes narrowing as his square jaw clenches tight. It's just a stool. I am not scared of sitting on a symbolic stool when I have done nothing wrong. 'In fact, the minister should have made you *stand* on the stool so that the whole congregation could see your sorry face. But I can see you aren't interested in repenting. You aren't sorry for what you are. And we all know what you are.'

'You have no idea what I am. Or who I am,' I say. I take a deep breath. Another twelve-year-old cannot frighten me.

He ignores me. 'You are a witch's daughter. Which means you too are a witch. Like mother, like daughter.'

I shrug, but my heart is thumping in my chest.

'Say it. Say, "I am a witch".'

The girls huddle together and giggle.

'Has your dead cat got your tongue?' asks Cecily. I look at her standing meekly behind Jack and I can't believe that we used to blow clouds away from the sun and swim in the river together. When the war started, we even learned to sword fight together. I can't believe Cecily used to be my best friend. I will not let her see me cry.

Jack turns to her and glowers.

'I'm waiting,' he says, kicking at the grass. 'Or are you

unable to speak without your animal familiar? What was your cat's name?'

I say nothing. I blink furiously to stop the tears.

'Malkin,' says Cecily softly.

'Ah, yes, Malkin,' says Jack. 'Poor *dead* Malkin. I hear she's inside the walls of your house. That you and your mother mummified her. You are so strange.'

Cecily, how could you?

Jack's smile reveals his yellowing teeth. 'We all know that the devil takes the form of dogs, mice, toads, hedgehogs, snakes … and, more often than not, a cat. A black cat.'

He takes a step forward, but I can see it in his eyes. It is he who is scared of me. He retreats and leans on the gravestone again.

'Why didn't the soldiers take you too, Art Flynt? Did you make yourself invisible? Trick them in some way using your magic, perhaps? Or did you simply poison them with your mother's bad magic herbs?'

'They are not magic. Those herbs are medicinal. They save lives.'

Jack grunts.

'You don't have a very good memory, Jack Norman,' I continue. 'My mother saved your brother with her medicine. He was all but dead from worms and Mother knew which herbs would revive him. You didn't call her a witch then, did you? As for you, Cecily, have you forgotten that your mother came running to mine for counsel when your father was delirious and babbling about his missing cows?'

Cecily's cheeks colour and she looks away.

'I have a good mind to drag you to the local magistrate myself,' says Jack, laughing under his breath and stepping towards me more confidently this time. 'I hear he pays up to a month's wages for turning in a witch.'

'Aye, if Art is still here tomorrow, I will come with you,

46

Jack,' says Cecily, looking me in the eye briefly. Her face is stony, but I am sure she is persuading Jack to wait. She is giving me time to decide.

'My mother says that witches are good at hiding their true selves,' says Jack. 'But you don't fool me. I see you. Although I would rather *not* see you. I think it's time you left Kelso on that beloved horse of yours . . .'

'Lady,' says Cecily, trying her best not to let Jack see that she is close to tears.

Jack scowls at her. Then he turns his attention back to me. 'No one wants you here, Flynt. Take Lady and leave.'

He turns away, walks towards the rusting iron gate and kicks it open. Cecily and the others trot obediently behind, giggling and whispering.

I let the oak support me, imagining its roots running deep into the earth.

I wish I could be in a place where I am unknown. Where I am not judged or mocked or excluded. Or, worse, pitied.

The sun splits heavy grey clouds apart and colours the sky orange and red. I pull the blanket more tightly around myself, but still I am cold. I run my tongue over my lips and taste the salty tears. Jack is right. No one wants me here. The town where I was born is no longer my home.

4

The pathway to the top of the hill is narrow and steep. Tree roots twist up from the soil and jagged stones point skywards. I stare at the ground, careful not to trip. Walking so fast that my breath becomes short and sharp, I force myself to listen to the high-pitched chitter-chatter of the male blackbird and the rattle of the mistle thrush as it flies high in the treetops. The mistle thrush sings come rain or shine. It even sings during storms. Cecily once told me that it sings in bad weather to defend its beloved holly bushes from bigger birds. The mistle thrush will confront buzzards and barn owls. It is not easily scared.

The trees give way to light and I blink for a moment, catching my breath. I stride through the sweet-smelling long grass until I reach a stone wall. The wall isn't very high, but I stand carefully on a flat grey stone, look out to the east and imagine I can see the blue of the sea beyond the ocean of trees. Below me, lochs glisten in the sun and burns twist and turn until they reach the coast. Somewhere beneath the canopy of trees are villages Father used to point out to me when we climbed this hill together. I have never visited them, but I remember them all: Holburn, Kimmerston, Elwick, Bamburgh. All villages in England.

Here, on the top of Sweethope Hill, I cannot see any signs of the war Mother wrote about in her letter. I don't know what war feels like, but I remember the day Cecily's eldest brother Dougie came back from battle, his face grey with exhaustion and his boots covered in mud flecked with blood. In the first week he was home, he told Cecily that the soldiers marched as if they were sleepwalking. He spoke of the dead being laid to rest in unmarked graves. And in the year since he has been home, he has never uttered another word.

Cecily's kind-hearted cousin Glenn, who came back from England six months after Dougie, slept for a week and then went back to work in the fields. Just after Christmas, when frost had painted the fields silver, Cecily and I waited for Glenn, jumping up and down on the crisp ground and puffing out white breath. As he walked back into Kelso, we flanked him, so that he might not escape. What was England like, we wanted to know. We knew the English used different words – a burn was in fact a stream – but did they *look* different?

Glenn laughed. 'We are certainly lucky living in Kelso. We don't have much, but we have enough.' And he told us stories of meeting a mother who begged him for a coin so that she might buy bread to feed her six children and of farmers guarding crops with guns. 'We heard stories that sounded made up,' he said. 'Neighbours turning against each other and betraying their families for a handful of coins.' When we pushed him for more information, he simply sighed. 'I don't know what else to tell you, girls. Everyone was very quick to accuse wives and mothers of being witches for money.'

A barn owl flies in front of me, its brown wings barely flapping, its ghostly white heart-shaped face focused intently on something hidden in the long grass.

'What are you looking for, wise owl?' I ask out loud, standing very still.

The owl is not interested in me, but if I move it will glide away. It lands on a nearby wall, its long legs like stilts. Mother wasn't at all sure that frogs could cure warts, but she believed that owls were both great protectors and bringers of prophecy.

My own mother, alone in the cart, unsure of her destiny.

My hair blows across my face and I tie it up with a piece of short string. The owl turns its head to look at me, its black eyes bright.

'I was born under this sky,' I tell the owl, before looking towards the sea. 'But everyone I love has been taken from me. My father, my sister, my brother and now ... Mother. Even my best friend Cecily has abandoned me. I fear a future unknown, but I don't want to stay here either. What should I do?'

Clouds race across the sky, casting fast-moving shadows on to the valley below. The owl stares at me, unblinking, before swivelling its head east and flying towards Holburn.

I know what I must do. I know I must leave.

5

It feels strange in the house without Mother. I used to tire of being told to do endless chores, but now I long for Mother to be standing in front of the fire, poking the logs back into life and teasing me about how slowly I always do things. I mustn't delay by thinking of the past, of the times that this house was full of laughter – I must prove that I can do things without always being told.

My stomach twists and my jaw clenches tight. I must think logically. I know I am not wanted in Kelso and Mother's letter did not instruct me to stay at home. She wrote about meeting my guides along the way; perhaps she even hoped I would follow her. After all, who else can save her?

Lady is saddled and ready in the stable, so I work out what I will need on my journey. There's only enough room for essentials in the saddlebags, so I pack the compass set in stone, a faded map of England, bread, cheese and a flask of water. Two coils of rope. Three of Mother's handkerchiefs. Her letter.

I want, more than anything, to go to Mother's room and hold her clothes to my face, to take comfort from her smell. How I loved her. How I *love* her.

Instead, I rummage around in the drawers in the corner of the kitchen and pull out Arthur's old clothes that I used to wear to help Mother clean the stables. I roll the sleeves of Arthur's shirt right up. His trousers are so big that I have to pull the belt tight to find the extra hole I made with the scissors and a stone. Finally, I attach Thomas's sword and knife to the belt.

I think of the girls in the graveyard, following Jack like obedient puppies. If I travel as a girl there will be questions asked, even by strangers. Girls must stay at home and not speak out of turn. They must be modest and meek and, when they marry, honour and obey. It is surely easier to be a boy in this world.

I take a pair of rusty scissors from the kitchen sink and stand in front of the polished stone on the dresser. Taking a deep breath, I bend over until my hair almost touches the floor. I carefully cut a handful of hair and put it by the sink. I cut and cut until a mass of brown curls lies on the

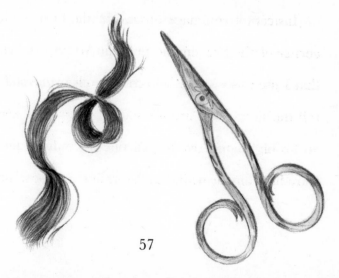

floor. As the curls hiss and burn on the embers of the fire, I watch part of myself die.

I peer into the polished stone and tentatively touch my ragged hair. Is that really me? I look just like Cousin Arthur, who is shy and thoughtful and who never sits still.

Yet here I am, standing in the middle of the kitchen on my own, dressed as a boy. *Looking* like a boy. All I have to do now is have the *authority* of a boy. I stand with my legs apart, my hands on my hips, my head held high.

'I am a boy,' I say. 'I am not afraid of anyone or anything.'

As I reach for the curl of hair by the sink and put it in my pocket to remind me of my old self, I catch another glimpse of myself in the polished stone, my roughly hacked hair, my stance, my courageous expression, and I laugh.

I look around the kitchen one last time. I pick up everything from the kitchen table. I am sure that is everything. The map, the food, Mother's letter … Mother's recipe book! How could I have almost forgotten it?

I tug at the drawer beneath the kitchen sink and push aside the knives and wooden spoons and bits of string. Nothing. *What if someone has taken the recipe book and burned it? Who would do such a thing?* But if they are happy to drown kittens and kill cats, then they are capable of anything. I step back and look at the sink. The second drawer that we never use. I pull at it, but it won't budge. I pull again and it eases open. There it is!

I take the small, battered recipe book out carefully and look through it. There, alongside Mother's intricate illustrations of all the herbs she loves, from archangel and white bedstraw to borage and blue bottle, are carefully written recipes. I hold the little book to my chest and then put it in the inside pocket of Arthur's overcoat, next to Mother's letter. It fits perfectly.

I recall fragments of Mother's letter. *You will not … be*

dragged under. What else? *Like any journey, it will begin with the first step.*

Leaving Kelso is the first step.

I take Thomas's treasured cap and pull it down so that my face is in shadow.

I turn to the front door, reach up and place my palms on the sealed cavity which, over time, has become smooth. 'Goodbye, sweet Malkin,' I whisper as I leave. 'Keep me safe on my journey to find Mother.'

6

We stand, my horse and I, among the ruins of Roxburgh Castle. I know I must leave in haste, but I want to see Kelso one last time. I look at the church spire glinting in the sun at the point where the two rivers meet. During the summer months, Cecily and I used to dare each other to leap off the slippery chalk banks and into the fiercely cold water. We would return home, damp and cold, our jaws chattering, and Mother would chastise us gently before sitting us in front of the fire and making us a warm drink.

I look down at the map, thankful that Father taught Thomas and me how to read maps when we were young. I have never even been to England and Essex seems so far away. Thomas and I always wondered if it would be different. If, as soon as we crossed the border, the air would somehow feel heavier and the grass wouldn't be so green or the sky so blue. If the people would speak strangely and look *other*.

I gaze at the places with their unfamiliar names, towns and villages that I might see at a distance or even pass through. Jedburgh. Consett. Easingwold. Selby. Coninsby. Brandon. Lavenham. Dedham. Manningtree. If I'm lucky and I don't get lost and no one tries to stop me, I can reach Essex in four days. Lady will, I know, try her very best to take me to Mother. I stroke her warm neck as she idly pulls at tufts of grass, her tar black stockings pulled up to her knees, a perfectly symmetrical white blaze extending from her eyes to her soft muzzle.

'Thank you very much for coming with me, Lady,' I say, pulling the strap on her saddle a little tighter. 'It is time.'

I mount her and press my left thigh on to her side so that she knows to turn away from Kelso. I walk Lady carefully down the rocky pathway from the castle to the road, which is flanked by trees. The road is empty, but I pull my cap down so that my face is in shadow. As we head east, the road twists and turns like the rivers and becomes narrower and narrower.

Lady tenses. She stops. I press her with both legs, yet she won't move. 'What is it, Lady?' I ask gently, but she just stares into the trees ahead. I distract myself by trying to remember what Mother taught me about the countryside. How, on a clear night, Orion's Sword can be seen pointing south; how drops of rain get smaller as the red in a rainbow fades or how animals point their tails in a certain direction to flag danger to each other. After

I ran away with the kittens, she told me time and again to respect the fields and the trees, to watch and listen and always be alert.

I can't see anything and all I can hear is the wind gently fanning the leaves. 'Let's go, Lady,' I whisper, even though there's no reason to whisper. Finally, she turns her head back to the road and walks forward, slowly, cautiously.

'There's nothing to be scared of. Nothing at all,' I say loudly, leaning to stroke Lady's black mane. 'At least you've had some grass. I'm starving and we cannot stop till nightfall, when we cross the border into England.'

Lady's ears flatten against her head.

'Oh, Lady, we shall never reach Essex if you keep stopping.'

There is a stirring in the bright green ferns that line the edge of the trees.

I sit as still as I can, trying not to let my hands shake.

The dense ferns are still for a moment, but then the fronds start to move again. A black tail appears, erect and flicking.

'Malkin?'

Someone coughs, a nasty, hacking cough that might benefit from Mother's rub. Liquorice, vinegar, treacle and rose water.

The cough is getting closer, but I don't want to lose sight of the cat's tail. The ferns are still. There is no tail to be seen.

Tails alerting danger.

I look up and there, ahead of us, is a man on his horse. The road is so narrow that one of us will have to stop to let the other pass.

A ditch separates the road and the trees on both sides. The man is moving closer, coughing so hard that his whole body convulses. I move Lady till she is on the edge of the ditch. My armpits prickle with sweat. I try to relax and not look suspicious. I peer below the peak of my cap. The man, I see now, is Alfred. He knew my father; they worked the fields together one summer before my brother Thomas died of typhus, before war broke out.

Alfred stops his chestnut horse just in front of me. 'Afternoon.' He points towards the trees. 'Folk talk of witches hiding in there.'

He must be able to hear my heart beating. He knows I am Agnes's daughter. He is playing a game. I nod.

'Aye, women might be the weaker vessel but they are capable of all nature of tricks, you mark my words.'

The weaker vessel! I stop myself from frowning. I have to say something. *I am not afraid of anything.* 'Yes, sir.'

'My crops are no better this year. I don't know how I'm going to feed my sons. Or my daughter. I am going to have to find another way of making money. Witch hunting, maybe.' He stops to cough. 'Are you heading for England?'

I freeze.

'I asked if you are heading towards England?'

I hold my breath. Nod again.

'It's risky in England, but as you were.' Alfred spits into the ditch and moves his horse on. 'Be careful, son.'

I let my breath out.

Son.

He thinks I am a boy. Mother was right. I will not be dragged under.

*

My first night in England is the first full night I have ever spent alone. When the sunlight has faded away, I find a small clearing in the forest and tie Lady to the thin trunk of a silver birch; I trust her not to leave me, but if she is startled by a bird or an animal, she might panic and canter away. I allow myself a small chunk of cheese and bread and a few sips of water. I slide down the gnarled, thickened trunk of an ancient ash, twisting and turning to get comfortable.

'I shall tell you a bedtime story to help you sleep,' I say to Lady, who is standing quietly, her eyes already closed. 'Once upon a time, there was a boy called Thomas who was desperate for a younger sister …'

I awake, startled. I must have fallen asleep for a minute, perhaps even an hour. The darkness is impenetrable and I can barely make out Lady's shape. My senses are heightened and I hear every tiny movement in the forest. Lady's soft, regular breath soothes me, but I can think only of Mother. Thoughts go round and round in my head: I don't know if I will be able to ride all the way to Essex on my own; I don't know if I'll be able to read the map properly; I don't know if I will be able to find more food; *I don't know if Mother is alive.*

I cry myself to sleep.

I am still exhausted upon awakening. As I ride south, I see that Thomas and I were wrong. The grass here is the same green, the sky the same vivid blue. The world is glorious. Mother *has* to be alive.

7

14 June 1647

Seven days to summer solstice

'Kill her!'

The voice is in the distance, but it's getting nearer. Panic travels up my body like a dark shadow. It's barely an hour past dawn and the air is not yet warm, but my shirt sticks to my clammy back. A buzzard glides overhead, a V-shaped silhouette against the pink sky. A *bad omen*. I watch it land softly on a rooftop and look down imperiously on the empty village square.

I should leave, but instinct tells me to stay.

Lady tenses beneath me. I grip her reins tightly so

she knows to
stay still, and
lean forward to
peer through the
empty market stalls.
A woman with bare feet runs
into the middle of the square, her
clothes torn, her face frozen in fear. I put my hand on my
sword. The woman looks wildly around the square.

She runs towards a door.

Locked.

She tries another.

The third opens. She stumbles into it and shuts it hard
behind her.

Six soldiers march into the square, their faces flushed.
They are dressed entirely in black, their upper bodies
protected with heavy armour. One points at the ground,
to the footsteps in the sawdust.

They follow the prints to the first door. To the second. Bile rises from my stomach. The woman is alone and will almost certainly be caught and I can do nothing. I clench my jaw. The tallest soldier launches himself at the third door, which opens easily. Five of the soldiers push their way into the house. The sixth takes a stub of white chalk from his pocket and scrawls a large 'W' on to the door. W *for witch*. He sweeps chalk dust from his trousers, broadens his shoulders and stands guard, his musket ready to fire.

I pull my cap down, turn Lady away from the square and keep to the shadows. As the narrow alleyway leads us further away, I bend over Lady's neck and inhale the familiar smell of sweat and grass. We are so close to the wall that my leg scrapes against it, leaving a streak of white dust on my trousers.

The alleyway finally opens out on to bright green fields and, in the distance, a line of trees. It promises to be a perfect spring day, but I am overwhelmed with guilt. I didn't try to save the woman from the soldiers and now …

'Could I have done something, Lady? Anything?'

She swings her head from right to left, as though in response. She's right. A girl dressed as a boy would never have had a chance against those soldiers.

Lady's ears flatten against her head. Her breathing is heavy, her nostrils flare. Just ahead of us, a small group of people have gathered around a placard nailed to a tree.

A thin boy with hollow eyes turns and looks up at me, squinting against the low sun.

'You'd better have a read of this if you're wanting to make proper money,' he says, his voice trembling with excitement.

I glance behind, towards the alleyway, but no one has followed me. My curiosity gets the better of me, so I dismount and push my way through the group to read the placard.

TO THE PEOPLE OF ENGLAND:
CAST OUT ALL WITCHES!

Witches are contaminating these parts. They may look like simple women, but they wear the mark of the devil. They offer potions. They speak out of turn. They are disobedient. They plot behind our backs. They are libertines who have sold their souls to the Lord of Hell.

GENEROUS REWARD
FOR PRESENTING THESE
EVIL SPIRITS TO THE
WITCHFINDER'S
SOLDIERS.

Printed by THE WITCHFINDER GENERAL, 1647

Alongside the Witchfinder General's goading words, there's a simple drawing of an old woman with a large nose and a bent back, leaning heavily on a walking stick, a black cat at her feet.

I stifle a laugh. I have never seen a woman with a bird's beak for a nose!

That is ridiculous, I think. The boy turns. I must have spoken out loud.

'Who are you?' he asks, ripping bits of bark off a long stick. 'I haven't seen you in Consett before. And your accent is unusual.'

Now that the talk is no longer of money, his voice is flat and his eyes hold no emotion.

'Aye, I am only passing through. I am on my way to meet my brother in …' I picture the map. 'Easingwold.'

'Might your brother be one of them?' He jerks his head towards the placard. 'A witchfinder?'

Be kind, Mother says. Always be kind.

76

I swallow my anger. 'Like everyone else in England, my brother is doing what he can to feed his family.'

'My father says he wouldn't delay in handing over women from the village who speak out of turn. When the soldiers arrived this morning, they already had a few dozen witches on their carts.'

My heart soars. 'Did you see a woman with long red hair and green eyes in one of them? She might have been on her own.'

He scratches his head furiously and I take a step back towards Lady, even though I know lice can't jump very far. 'All the witches I saw had short hair.' He frowns. 'Why are you so interested in a witch with red hair?'

'I'm not,' I say quickly, my heart beating faster. 'I just heard that the ones with red hair and green eyes are the most … powerful.'

'I understand. If that is the case, they will also be worth the most money. Thank you for the tip.'

You fool, Art Flynt. You have just thoughtlessly alerted the boy to your mother.

He wanders away through the grass, his skinny legs forming an O-shape as he drags his stick behind him.

As I mount Lady, my mind is flooded with conflicting thoughts. If this is England, I don't want to be here. I don't want to meet people so desperate they are willing to send women to their deaths for a few coins. I don't want to be forced to tell a stranger that my mother is a bigger prize than other women. I would rather travel in silence. I cannot go back to Kelso. Besides, why would I go back to Scotland? I have no friends there. No real family. *Always believe in your destiny,* Mother wrote in her letter. I sit up straight. I must not feel sorry for myself. Mother is alone, in a cart. I have Lady.

I think of Mother holding her moonstone necklace up to the sun, its rainbow colours catching the light. 'One day this sacred stone will be yours,' she used to say. 'My mother – your grandmother – gave it to me; it is the stone of the mother moon and protects you whenever you travel.'

'Let the moonstone keep Mother safe in England, Lady,' I shout, as we gallop through endless fields of wild grass.

8

15 June 1647

Six days to summer solstice

I continue south, putting as much distance as possible between myself and Kelso. Mother calmed herself with nature and so must I. The sharp, musky smell of fox fills the forest. Shards of moonlight push down through the trees and illuminate the endless ranks of silver birch, gently bending towards each other. As Lady trots over dry branches, they snap like brittle bones. I keep my head low to avoid branches until the trees finally give way to fields. Lady pauses. She holds her head high, snorts and breaks out into a canter. I align my spine with hers and soon we are racing through the tall, damp grass again.

As night becomes day, the darkness drifts away and the sky is streaked red ochre and dark pink. Mist hangs low in the fields. It's so beautiful that I forget. I forget about Thomas, about Father and even, for a short time, about Mother. I forget about Cecily's betrayal, about Jack taunting me and my aunt treating me with contempt. I forget that I am alone, and scared. I feel free, as though my body is suffused with light. If nobody knows who I am, nobody can judge me.

The feeling of freedom is fleeting. I miss home. I miss baking bread with Mother and the feel of flour caked on my skin when Mother painted my face with the leftovers, both of us laughing as my skin became paler than ever.

A large cloud casts a shadow across the field and I suddenly feel cold. Lady slows down. The sound of gunshot echoes around the nearby fields. Lady rears up. I sit forward and loosen the reins. Her ears flick back and forth impatiently.

'We are safe, Lady,' I whisper, patting her neck, but my voice is unsteady. It must have been a soldier. Most likely more than one. Have they come to find me? Surely even Aunt Elizabeth, with her heart of stone, would not want me to be taken? Not Alfred; he seemed to think I was a boy. Not the thin boy in Consett; I doubt he thought he could make any money out of me.

I look across the fields, but they are empty and silent once more. I turn Lady in the direction of a patch of trees sitting atop a hillock and, from the safety of the trees, survey the fields below. I strain my eyes to check the adjacent fields, which appear to be empty. It must be safe to ride back down the hillock.

BANG!

BANG!

BANG!

A flurry of gunshots. I pat Lady's neck to calm her. A dozen soldiers appear on horseback, cantering along the far side of the field.

I freeze.

'Don't move, Lady,' I whisper. 'Not an even an inch.' Lady stands as still as a statue.

I am close enough to see the determination on the soldier's faces as they race towards the gap in the overgrown summer hedge.

Please don't turn. Don't look across the field, towards the hillock.

I hold my breath and grip Lady's reins so tight that

my fingers turn white. Another shot, so close that it seems to shake the trees. I don't breathe. Lady doesn't move.

The sky is filled with a mass of burned-orange-and-black birds. Pheasants! *They were shooting birds!* I feel dizzy with relief.

When I am sure all the men have gone, with the birds flung over the horses' necks, I trot Lady up and down the field, trying to find a pheasant for myself. I'm about to give up when I spot one tangled in the hedge, its shimmering copper plumage still bright, but its body limp. We shall find a good place to make an overnight camp and I shall dine like royalty!

*

By early evening, Lady is flagging and I can't stop thinking of the pheasant cooking slowly over a fire on a stick. We stop by a burn and I allow Lady to stand in the shallow water and drink to her heart's content. As exhausted as I feel, I must practise before eating. The hilt of my sword is decorated with an elaborate mass of twisted silver, like a nest of skinny snakes. Remembering what Thomas taught me, I slip my right hand into the hilt, bend my right knee and lunge forward, stabbing and cutting the air with the long, thin blade. I think of the soldiers who took Mother away. I think of the man in the square, wiping the chalk dust off his hand before standing guard while his friends killed a woman who was almost certainly innocent. I lunge forward again, growling, imagining the tip of my sword at the soldier's throat, his chalky hands raised in defeat.

My right shoulder aches, but I want to be – I have to be – stronger, fiercer, faster. I twist and turn, thrusting the sword relentlessly, until my face is hot and sweat drips off my eyebrows and my upper lip. Lady wanders out of the burn and stands in the shade of the trees, her eyes half-shut, her neck and lips drooping, ignoring me.

The sword becomes heavier and heavier. The jabs

become half-hearted and my growls turn into whimpers. With one last show of strength, I plunge the sword into the hard ground. 'I bid the pox on you and your fellow soldiers!'

I kick off my boots and stand barefoot in the middle of the shallow burn, allowing the bracing water to refresh me. The stones are smooth and comforting beneath my tired feet. I close my eyes and let my body sway in the breeze.

I hear Cecily's voice: *Step into the deeper water. I dare you.* The stones beneath my feet feel jagged, as though they have teeth. The water feels freezing cold. I open my eyes and fall against the bank of the burn, clawing at the tangled roots of a black willow tree.

I wrap my wet arms around Lady's neck. 'Did you hear Cecily too? Or am I delirious with hunger? There is plenty of wood around here and it's dry enough to start a fire. I shall pluck the pheasant and cook it on a spit. I shall pick some dandelions for you so that you can join me in the feast, Lady.'

*

The carpet of luminous green moss is soft and springy. I watch the bats hurtling through the air and the badgers stalking the forest floor, collecting earthworms and nuts. My stomach is full and my eyelids are heavy.

Thomas and I are in the dense forest where I took the sack of kittens. He is waiting to go to war and he is as strong as he has ever been. A few weeks later, typhus fever will kill him, but for now he is bursting with life. He is showing me how to lunge, how to take a quick step, how to balance. A pair of Duke of Burgundy butterflies float by, their orange-and-brown wings vibrant against the green trees. I watch them alight on the tip of a fern, so close together that they blur into one another.

'Art, focus. In the moment you lost concentration, your opponent could have pushed his sword into your body. You would now be dead.' His voice is kind but grave. He picks his sword up, challenging me

to a return match. All I can hear is the sharp clang of my sword meeting his over and over and over again. 'Thomas, please, we must stop, I'm exhausted.' He shakes his head and I am sure that I will collapse. 'You are nearly as good as me now, wee sister,' he laughs, leaning his sword against a tree and wiping his brow. 'But not quite.' I feel his strong arm around my shoulder, and we walk back to the house in an easy silence.

'Thomas,' I mumble, half-asleep. 'I will work hard to be as good as you …'

I put my hand firmly on my sword, lean back against a tree and let my body sink down into the soft, sweet-smelling earth.

9

16 June 1647

Five days to summer solstice

I am balancing on the milking stool, staring out of the attic window.
The window is black and I rub and rub with my sleeve, harder and
harder but still I can't see. I wrap my fist in my shirt and break the
window. The soldiers are shouting. One woman is to be saved. They
are looking up at me and laughing. I can't see the women. I can't
see Mother.

I awake from the nightmare with a jolt. I know at once
that I am not alone. I open my eyes just enough to see.
First only the embers from the fading fire and the outlines
of trees in the shadowy light. I hold my breath. All I can

hear is my heart and all I can see is Lady, her hind leg slightly bent in her resting position.

I adjust my eyes to the early morning light. My hip feels bruised from lying curled up on my side on the hard ground. *One woman is to be saved.* I turn carefully on to my back.

A woman is staring down at me.

I must still be dreaming.

I close my eyes and open them again slowly to be sure I'm not seeing things. The woman's head is a mass of black curls, her long velvet dress a deep, dark purple. She is as old as Mother and quite beautiful. She looks at me carefully, her eyes changing from brown to green and back again as the sun pushes through clouds.

I am on my feet within seconds, my hand on my sword. The woman smiles and I see that one of her front teeth is missing.

'Please don't be scared. You have no need to leave. I

shall go if you wish. I saw you and your horse sleeping and I wanted to wish you well on your journey.' She extends her hand. 'My name is Maude.'

I look at her hand for a moment before shaking it warily. Her handshake is firm, her skin smooth and warm.

'I have been waiting for you. I knew you would come, I just didn't know when.'

How could she possibly have known?

'What is your name?' she asks softly.

Don't give anything away.

I stare at the ground.

'You don't have to tell me,' Maude says eventually. 'But may I ask where you and your gentle horse are going?'

I have to say something, but I don't want to lie in case she asks questions that I can't answer.

'Essex. We are going to Essex.'

'I know nothing of what you have seen since you left Scotland,' she says, the tenderness in her voice replaced by an urgency. 'But you will witness bloodshed. You will see hatred between men and women who were once neighbours. I have seen people betray each other. Husbands forsaking their wives and men their daughters.'

'How do you know I'm from Scotland?' I ask, suddenly conscious of my voice.

She smiles. 'You have a very soft Scottish accent. But never mind that. I foresaw troubled times before the civil war started. Men were scornful of my prediction – how would a woman know about war? But the local women had grown to trust me and were more inclined to listen.'

She pauses and adjusts the bright red scarf around her neck. 'Some say I am wise, but I was slow to realise that I live in a village full of mercenaries, even though I have long been regarded with suspicion. All my life I have been judged for preferring my left hand over my right.

When I was a child, my parents tied my left arm behind my back, hoping I would use my right hand.'

'Aye, folk believe that being left-handed is a path to Satanism,' I say.

Maude nods. 'People blindly accept what they are told. It is the way of the world. It is hard to know who to trust.'

'You remind me . . .'

'Of your mother? Tell me about her.'

I tell the stranger standing in front of me that Mother prescribed herbal remedies to people in our town and beyond: comfrey roots for fever, gout and broken bones; dandelion root for a woman's monthly bloated stomach.

'My mother always had advice, for folk who sought it,' I add. '*Every day is a journey.* What else? *Swim with the tide, not against it.* She was . . .' I stop. 'She is widely respected . . .' Without warning, the sobs rise up from my stomach. I double over in pain.

'I have to find my mother.' I swallow hard. 'I have to believe she is alive.'

Breathe. One, two, three. One, two, three. I must believe. Mother is alive.

'Do not grieve for that which has yet to come to pass,' says Maude, stepping forward to rest her hand on my shoulder.

My throat tightens. 'That is easy for you to say. It is not your mother whose fate hangs in the balance.' Shame heats my face. 'I'm sorry. Please tell me what you know.'

Maude removes her hand from my shoulder. She looks behind her quickly, as though expecting someone. 'I don't have much time. Listen carefully: beware of the man who calls himself the Witchfinder General and trust only those who stand in his way. You will come across him soon enough. He wears a tall hat and an English pointer is always at his side.'

'The Witchfinder General? I know of him. The minister spoke of him in church and as soon as I crossed from Scotland into England, I saw a placard offering a reward for the capture of witches.'

'And you will see many more. I noticed his men nailing up more placards this very morning. He is no doubt issuing orders from his castle just outside Manningtree. His war on so-called witches is gathering momentum.'

She puts her hand deep into her pocket.

She pulls out a long, thin silver chain with a stone attached to it and quickly tightens her fist around it.

'You will not be able to rescue your mother alone. You will not have to. In the meantime, this amulet is for you. It will not only help you on your journey, but it will also bring you good fortune. If you believe in it, it will offer you protection. Above all else, believe in its agency.'

'Its agency?'

'Its power. Value the amulet and safeguard it at all times.'

She opens her palm and the rainbow colours of the moonstone flash in the sunlight.

'But that's Mother's moonstone!' I exclaim. As long as I can remember, Mother used to hold her moonstone up to the light to show me its wonderfully shimmering colours.

'Put it around your neck, child, and keep it hidden.'

'Did you steal it from Mother? Did you meet her? Is this a trick?'

Maude shakes her head. 'It is *your* amulet. Trust me.'

As though in a trance, I put the amulet around my neck and tuck it under my shirt. It is cool against my chest.

Maude continues. 'Before I go, remember this: the answer to your dilemma is to be found among the horses. You will find the truth when you are at the river's flow. The river ends with twists and turns.'

Goosebumps rise on my arms. 'Mother used to talk of *watching* a river's flow.'

'A wise woman indeed,' says Maude, adjusting her scarf.

'But I don't understand what being at the river's flow means,' I say.

'I must take my leave. Onwards, child. Always onwards.' Before I can protest, she is lost among the shadows of the forest.

10

I touch the stone and it is oddly warm, as though it has been lying in the blazing sun rather than inside my shirt, as though it is somehow alive. Is that what Maude meant when she told me to believe in the amulet's agency?

Onwards, she said. *Always onwards.*

I inspect the map and continue my journey south-east towards Lavenham, Dedham and Manningtree.

I dare not take my eyes off the forest pathway in case another horse approaches, but the few riders I pass are always young men who simply nod in my direction and make no eye contact. Each time I am thankful that my disguise is working.

I want to keep going, but steam is rising off Lady and I can feel panic flooding my body again. We stop by a shallow burn far enough from the pathway to be hidden from view and I allow her to linger, her muzzle dipping into the water to drink.

I am distracted by a damselfly skimming the surface of the water, weaving backwards and forwards, its bright blue body transported by four veined wings.

I sit by the burn, just for a moment, and scoop cool water up in my hands, gulping it down and splashing my face. The air is warm and clear and the sun directly overhead. The morning has already gone! I must make haste. Lady sets off through the trees at a pace, fortified by her time idling by the water. The forest is humid and the rich smell of ancient earth mingles with the delicate scent of summer flowers. When the trees give way to a large clearing, I signal to Lady to stop so that I can check for any signs of human life. My elevated position gives me a slight advantage, but I feel uneasy, as though my bad dream has bled into reality.

A piece of rope sways gently in the wind. I look around the clearing again. I can see no one, hear no one. I slide off Lady's back and walk towards the rope, my hand on the hilt of my sword. It's not a rope, but a noose. I feel as though somebody has punched me hard in the stomach.

I turn to mount Lady so that we can canter out of here. But she has gone.

'Lady!' I shout urgently. 'Lady, where are you?'

I take the amulet out of my shirt and hold it in my palm, my fist against my chest. I follow the path, looking frantically into the trees. Just before the trees start to thin out, something catches my eye. The trees are so dense that the shape looks formless. My heart crashes in my chest. I tear at my nails with my teeth. The creature is standing completely still, its nose in the air. It looks too slight to be Lady, but I can't be sure. I daren't move in case I scare it and yet I can't stand there, wasting time. I move forward, carefully, silently. The animal moves too. I can see now that its antlers were lost in the shadow. Impressive though he is, a stag is of no use to me.

I kiss the moonstone. *Please. Help me. I can't do this on my own. I need Lady.*

I put the amulet inside my shirt again and put my head in my hands.

Lady, come back to me.

Something nudges me in the back. I spin around and see the large black eyes of my horse gazing at me.

'Lady!' I take her soft muzzle in my hands and kiss it. This time, my tears are not of sadness, but of joy and relief.

I take a brush from the saddlebag and groom her slowly and firmly, until her tar black stockings gleam and the blaze on her muzzle is as white as snow. It seems like such a long time ago we stood together looking at the rivers of Kelso.

'Thank you for coming back to me,' I say, kissing her muzzle.

The air is strangely still and heavy; rain will surely come soon. I mount Lady and put a hand on her soft mane. 'Now take me away from here as fast as you can.'

*

The land in Suffolk is flat and warm and a salty wind swirls across the marshy land. It is strange to ride across such low ground when I am so used to the cliffs and peaks of Kelso. Even stranger to be connected to Mother by these roads, which I am sure she travelled before me, her hands tied, her freedom taken away by the soldiers who stole her from me. I inhale deeply and breathe in the fresh air for her.

I am crazed with tiredness. I feel my eyelids closing until the jolt of Lady galloping awakens me.

Lady stops suddenly. We have reached the end of the track. Just ahead of us is a split in the path, one track forking to the left and the other to the right. I have no idea which to choose. I could look at the map but it would be useless, showing as it does, only the larger roads.

Lady turns to look into the trees. Moving back and forth among the long grasses is a tail in silhouette.

'Malkin,' I whisper. 'Is that you?'

The tail is too bushy. I am weak with exhaustion; my mind is playing tricks on me. Malkin is above the doorway at home, where she will always be.

A fox trots out of the trees, her orange tail held high. She stops in the middle of the track, lifts her snout and sniffs the air, whiskers twitching. The black tip of one of her ears is torn. She is so close I can smell her bitter scent. Lady snorts and the fox turns, as though noticing us for the first time. She looks at me, amber eyes unblinking.

Mother used to say that a single fox crossing your path is good luck.

'Which way should I go, Mrs Fox?'

She lifts a hind leg to scratch her ear.

How foolish to think that a fox could understand me.

The fox opens her mouth and slowly yawns. She trots to the end of the track, turns to look at us then turns right.

We follow her until she saunters off into the trees.

Am I to trust a fox?

I stop Lady and look around for another sign. Anything.

Lady paws the ground. I look down. On the road are three pheasant feathers. One long and two short, joined together in the shape of an arrow, pointing to the east.

'That will do, Lady,' I say. 'Let us ride till dusk and then we can find somewhere safe to sleep.'

11

17 June 1647

Four days to summer solstice.

The early morning sun burns away the mist from the marshes. The air is warm, the water is still and hawks drop noiselessly through the air to pluck their prey from the long grass. I allow myself a moment to sit and watch, to breathe deeply and think myself lucky to be alive. But when the sun disappears, I shiver and my mood darkens. I miss Mother so much that it hurts. Oh, to smell lavender and woodsmoke in her clothes. I take one of her handkerchiefs from my pocket and inhale her fading smell. She is with me, but she is gone.

I must make haste once more, though I am unable to move.

'Another sorry night's sleep,' I say, running my fingers through Lady's tangled mane. 'I don't suppose you noticed how damp the woods outside Lavenham were … and there is no more bread or cheese.'

Lady lifts her head and snorts.

'Are you saying we should go back to Kelso? What are you saying? Is that a yes? A no?' Lady starts walking. 'Where are you taking me?'

I relax the reins and let Lady guide me. She walks south, her head held high.

*

The trees are so dense that I have to dismount and guide Lady on foot. She stops with no warning and her ears flatten against her head.

'We're safe here, Lady. You're just spooked by the trees standing so close together.' I shiver. 'There hasn't been any sunlight here for a long time.'

I walk slightly ahead, pulling gently at her reins, but her hooves are planted firmly in the damp earth. I stop and listen. No birdsong. No animal sounds. Something is wrong, but it makes no sense to waste time by going back.

A crow flaps noisily out of the trees and my heart leaps. Lady's ears prick up.

'Is that what was bothering you, Lady?' I say, laughing with relief. 'It was just a crow! We need to push on. You may be satisfied with grass and dandelions, but I need more than berries and nuts to sustain me. It feels like weeks since I cooked that pheasant. I've already had to make two holes in my belt to tighten it.'

I start walking again and Lady follows. 'All the things we've seen and you are scared of a bird!'

We ride and ride, through long grasses and marshy land, disturbing wildlife as we go: brightly coloured damselflies, wading curlews with their curved bills and long, blue-tinged legs and, very occasionally, a bittern moving silently through the reeds until the male announces itself with its boom-like song over and over.

I concentrate on navigating the marshes until the land becomes firmer. Men on horses trot past and I force myself to sit up straight and nod as they pass, hoping my cap is throwing a shadow over my tired, disheartened face. Perhaps it is lucky that I am so hungry as I can think of little else. I pick apples as red as blood from a roadside tree and gorge on them till I feel sick. I think about bread warm from the oven and cheese as soft as clouds. I am so dizzy with hunger that I let go of the reins and hold on to the saddle for balance, allowing Lady to steadily follow the River Stour towards Dedham.

After Dedham, three miles along the river to Manningtree.

And, in Manningtree, the castle.

And, in the castle, the Witchfinder General.

You will not be able to rescue your mother alone. You will not have to.

The lack of food is making me hallucinate. I grab the reins and sit up. I look around me. I cannot see Maude, but I swear I heard her voice, as clear as the nightingale at dawn. On the road ahead, there is only an empty cart bouncing along the road towards Dedham and behind, a burly farmer herding an unruly flock of goats.

*

When I arrive at the next village, I see a sign for the Sun Inn tavern and tie Lady up outside. Once I'm sure no one is nearby, watching, I put Mother's letter, her recipe book and embroidered purse in one saddlebag and Arthur's coat in the other and hide them with my sword behind a tall bale of hay.

Church bells ring as I enter the square, as though announcing my arrival. I pull my cap down and walk into the village with my eyes cast down. Stalls upon stalls of

115

produce, and nobody here trying to sell it. I thank the moonstone for bringing me luck after all. Looking over my shoulder, I slip cheese, bread and two bright yellow quinces into my pockets and, hungry enough to risk being seen, I stand there and gorge on a pie that is still warm from the oven.

The church bells settle back into stately silence. In the distance, jubilant shouts are followed by edgy laughter.

The stolen food is heavy in my pockets. The shouting is ever louder. Fear and excitement hang in the air. I hesitate, just for a moment.

I should go back to Lady and leave. But there are four days till summer solstice, surely I can spend a few minutes here to see what the celebration is?

As soon as I leave the square, I see a huddle of people standing on a stone bridge. I join the edges of the crowd, hoping that no one will notice that I am a stranger. A girl's slender body lies curled up on the narrow wall of the bridge. The air is still oppressively warm and yet I feel as though I've walked into the middle of a freezing lake. A rope is loose around her neck; her right thumb tied to her left big toe; her dress is ripped. She is young, perhaps even younger than me, maybe ten years old.

A man is talking in a loud, pompous voice. His beard is short, his long hair lustrous beneath a tall hat. A red cape falls just short of his bucket-top boots. An elegant dog stands next to him, held tight on a velvet lead. The man is neither handsome nor ugly, but I am instantly repelled by his very presence.

A tall hat. An English pointer by his side. A group of guards. I had not expected to see him so soon.

My throat constricts.

It is him. The Witchfinder General. The self-appointed executioner.

He points vaguely at the girl's face and says triumphantly, 'Mercy West has witch marks. Clear as day. Warts!'

He takes a breath and continues. 'She has been seen offering boiled urine and hair in a stone bottle to children with scarlet fever and smallpox. She has confessed! We shall now prove she is a witch. If she sinks then she is innocent. If she floats then I shall be proved right: the water will have rejected her as a servant of the devil.'

The crowd jeers. 'Witch! Witch!'

A smaller man emerges from the Witchfinder General's shadow and slowly lowers Mercy towards the black water on a rope. She thrashes about helplessly.

'Please, don't drown me, please,' she begs, her blonde hair falling over her face. The man betrays no emotion.

I am paralysed. I look around for guidance. Surely I can't be the only one who wants to help? But all eyes are on the river. Men and women. Boys and girls, as young as four or five.

Out of the corner of my eye, I see three figures in flowing black cloaks emerge from the village square and

I turn to see them walking towards the crowd in long, confident strides, their faces obscured by billowing hoods. One holds a musket, the other a sword, the third a wooden longbow with a quiver of what looks like home-made arrows slung across his back. They huddle tightly together, whispering and pointing at the bales of hay that stand between the other end of the bridge and the road out of the village.

No one turns to look at them; the girl's imminent death is still mesmerising everyone on the bridge.

Clouds glide past the sun and my head starts to pound – a sure sign that a storm is approaching.

I should leave while I still can, before anyone notices me.

When Mercy's body hits the water, the man in the tall hat turns his back towards the crowd. He takes a small bow. The villagers clap.

I think of Maude. Of the woman running across the square. Of the women who were dragged from my house.

Of Mother. Trophies, all of them. *I can't let her drown.*

I pull the handkerchief up over the lower part of my face and my cap down so that only my eyes are visible, and I jump on to the stone wall. It's narrow and uneven, but my balancing skills are excellent. I move sideways, like an oversized yet elegant crab. The rope is tied to an old metal hook on the bridge and my first instinct is to cut the rope with my knife, but I wouldn't have time, and even if I did, Mercy West's hand is tied to her foot and she would drown more quickly.

I look up. Hopkins still has his back to me, basking in the applause. A scruffy brown dog barks and circles with excitement.

The three cloaked figures are walking shoulder to shoulder towards the other end of the bridge. *Can't they help me?* Hopkins turns towards me. A metallic taste fills my mouth. Fear. His smile disappears. His lip rises into a furious snarl and he is close enough for me to see his flinty

grey eyes harden and his alabaster skin flush red.

'Stop that boy!' he yells, pointing at me. 'He is a servant of Satan!'

You will find the truth when you are at the river's flow.

A flood of adrenaline courses through my body. I push the hanky down, tip my body backwards and fall into the river.

*

The crowd gasps as I tumble. I hit the water hard and open my eyes, catching my cap before it floats away and tucking it into my belt. The girl is suspended under the water, her long blonde hair diffused, tiny bubbles rising from her nostrils.

I reach for my knife and cut the rope around her neck, then take a deep breath and submerge myself in the water to cut the rope attaching her hand to her foot. I hook my arm around her slender neck and swim to the surface. Her skin is turning a pale blue. I glance up at the bridge.

The villagers are looking down on me from above, baying for my blood. Hopkins is nowhere to be seen, but I know he is coming for me.

A musket is fired. And then again. The villagers, distracted by this new commotion, turn around. Acrid smoke hovers above them. Arrows fly through the air.

'Stay with me! Please stay alive!' I whisper. The narrow river is lined by clumps of light green reeds and, beyond, a dense hedge of brambles. Holding the girl's limp body as tightly as I can around the chest, I pull her through the water, doing my best to avoid the reeds, until we reach the bridge.

The blackened underside of the bridge is carpeted with moss. I am used to the icy rivers in Kelso, but this water feels brutally cold. My legs pedal furiously underwater. I feel trapped, but I dare not move. Not yet.

Focus. Stay strong. I will not be dragged under.

I use all my strength to keep her head above the

water and feel for a pulse on her neck.

Thud.

Thud.

And then, just a flutter. Her heart is giving up.

Above me, an endless dull rumble. A stampede. Footsteps and hooves. I swallow a mouthful of silty water. Gunfire. A flurry of arrows flies off the bridge and floats gently down the river, its sting removed. The clash of metal. A high-pitched scream. Men shouting frantic instructions over one another.

'You must not die in my arms,' I whisper, holding the girl tight. 'Please, Mercy West. Don't die.'

12

Staying as close as I can to the bank of the river, I pull

Mercy through the water to the other side of the bridge

and hide among the tall, slender reeds. The clouds are

moving fast and low across the iron grey sky. People are

still shouting on the bridge and I'm sure I can hear the

sound of bleating, but I can't see anything; the bridge

is shrouded in smoke. The sweet smell of burning hay

mingles with the bitter musket smoke. I pull up the wet

hanky to muffle my coughing.

I let the water carry us downstream until the river

starts to twist away from the village. I hook my arm around Mercy's neck and use the other arm to hold on to a low-lying branch. As the smoke clears from the bridge, I see a small group of farmers frantically attempting to bring the burning bales of hay under control. Kid goats run along the narrow wall as nanny and billy goats charge at the villagers, their heads down. The Witchfinder General is in the distance, being led to safety by soldiers.

In the middle of the bridge, between the burning hay and the rampaging goats, one of the mysterious cloaked figures darts from side to side, taunting villagers with his sword, pushing them back towards the village square. There's a rumble in the distance. A crack of thunder. Lightning dances on the horizon.

Keep moving. Keep moving.

The muddy riverbank is slippery, but it's the only way out. I push Mercy up the bank, until she is half out of the water. I climb around her, sliding back into the freezing

water once, twice, a third time. I hold on to the branch so tightly that it starts to creak as if it will snap, but I finally manage to pull myself out. Using all the strength I can muster, I haul Mercy on to the damp grass and put my cap back on. I pull her limp body through the brambles, ignoring the tiny thorns as they catch on my clothes and draw pinpricks of blood from my hands.

Keep moving. Keep moving. We must move far away from the river.

I stand for a moment to catch my breath and put my hand inside my shirt to feel for the moonstone. It is cold and wet, but at least it is not lost. I can feel its protection, its *agency*.

'Stop, traitor!'

A short, stocky man has appeared from nowhere. He stands firmly in our way, his feet wide apart, arms crossed. My heart beats hard. A butterfly flutters past, but I barely notice it.

Suddenly he tips his head back and leers at me, before reaching for his sword and lurching forward. I am too quick for him. I step to the side so that he takes a moment to regain his balance. He lunges towards me and his sword catches my leg, but only rips the material. I jump backwards and he advances. I shall have to get really close to him to be able to use my knife.

Think fast!

I look over his shoulder and gasp. 'The Witchfinder!' As he turns, I step forward, thankful for my long legs, and my knife is quickly at his exposed throat. I put pressure on it. He starts to choke and splutter, stumbling backwards, his face flushed with a mixture of anger and embarrassment at falling for such a simple trick.

'Please, I have … I have a f … f … family,' he splutters.

'I will spare your life, but you must go.'

He stands there, making no attempt to move.

'Immediately,' I say. 'Go. Now.'

'Y … y … yes. Th … thank you.'

He straightens up and almost falls into a cluster of thistles before he dares to turn around and fight his way through the bracken.

I am still staring into the bracken when I notice the sound of retching. I spin around. Mercy, her face ashen, is sitting and coughing up murky water from the river. I kneel beside her, pat her back gently and take a leaf out of her hair, but she tries to wriggle away. Her breath is ragged and her eyes, as blue as cornflowers, are unblinking.

'My name is Art Flynt,' I say, extending my hand. She ignores it, her teeth chattering. 'We have to go. I can take you with me and leave you in a safe, warm place.'

'Art is an odd name for a boy.'

'I am not a boy,' I say, taking off my cap and forgetting

that my hair is cut short. 'We have to leave.'

She shakes her head. 'I am not coming with you.'

'I don't think you are safe here,' I protest.

I put my cap back on, rummage around in my pockets and offer her a quince. She grabs it without looking at me and takes a bite.

'Get away from me,' she hisses through a mouthful.

'Don't be scared,' I say, standing up. 'There's no need. I am on your side.'

Another crack of thunder and large drops of rain start dropping from the sky. We are both shivering, both still soaked through from the river.

Her mouth forms a crooked, suspicious smile. 'I am truly thankful that you saved me, but I presume you will now hand me back to the soldiers for a handful of coins …'

'Never!' I say, surprised by the force of my denial. 'I am on your side. I have travelled all the way from Scotland to bring down the Witchfinder General!'

She looks at me with wide eyes and a slack jaw.

'I feel terrible,' she says, her words barely audible.

'Wait a moment,' I say, before pointlessly adding, 'Stay there.'

Remember. Remember Mother's recipe book. Herbs for sickness. Elderflower. There are no trees nearby. What else? Wild spearmint!

The bushes are thorny, but I push them apart and crouch down, looking desperately for the bright green leaves.

Yes! There it is, right by the river, its leaves unbowed by the heavy rain.

I rip off a dozen leaves and run back to the girl.

'Put these on your forehead,' I say firmly.

She looks at me suspiciously, but takes the handful of spearmint leaves.

'How did you know ...?' she asks.

'It's not important. It will ease the pain in your head

132

soon enough and then we have to leave.'

She holds the leaves to her forehead for a few minutes, until the colour returns to her face. I help her to her feet and she stands there, swaying unsteadily, shivering and looking uncertain.

'Are you coming with me?' I ask, as gently as I can. 'I left my saddlebags hidden close to my horse; you can borrow my blanket to keep warm.'

She looks up at me at me and nods, her eyes full of tears. 'I am not used to the kindness of strangers.'

*

Mercy walks so slowly that I have to keep stopping and waiting for her. It's raining heavily now and our clothes are stuck to our bodies. Eventually I put my arm around her shoulders so that she can lean on me.

We circle the edge of the village in silence, both of us shivering uncontrollably. I am sure we are being watched, but whenever I turn around, I cannot see a soul.

This isn't the time for imagining things. I need to be strong for both of us.

Lady stands under the tavern's wooden awning, oblivious to the cruelty of humans. Her neck is soft and warm and I allow myself to hold her tight for a moment, expel all the stale air from my lungs and take several deep breaths. I pull my saddlebags from behind the hay and return my sword to its sheath. I wrap my blanket around Mercy's slender shoulders and carefully put Mother's letter, recipe book and purse back in the inside pocket of my coat. I am glad of its warmth and to have Mother's belongings close to me once more.

Voices drift out of the tavern's open windows.

'I am afraid,' says Mercy, her voice shaking. 'They will kill us both.'

'Not if we leave now,' I say, trying to sound more confident than I feel. 'I'm sure we can find somewhere to hide.'

I stroke Lady to calm myself.

'Hold on to the saddle firmly,' I say, giving her a leg-up on to Lady and sitting behind her.

I turn Lady away from the village and kick her gently, but she seems to know we must make haste. As we canter out of Dedham, the air thick with rain, Mercy mutters something. I lean forward to hear her.

'I know a safe place,' she whispers. 'Thank you for saving my life. I will do anything for you. Anything.'

13

The storm has passed and the damp forest smells of rich, fresh earth. Mercy raises her left hand and I tug Lady's reins so that we pull up quickly. She slides gracefully off Lady, dropping to her knees on the muddy ground. She pushes the wet leaves and twigs away and puts her ear to the ground.

'No one has followed us,' she announces triumphantly, a huge grin lighting up her face.

'Finally some good news,' I say, giggling for the first time in weeks.

I pull Mercy back on to the saddle and we ride onwards, deep into the forest, Lady's hooves flattening leaves and snapping fallen branches. We canter past ferns with light green fronds, pale pink dog rose and sweet-smelling honeysuckle, wild strawberries and common sorrel, ancient stones carpeted in lichen.

'Left here,' Mercy says and I guide Lady with the reins.

In front of us stands an abandoned house, its roof sagging, its dark windows staring out like blank, hostile eyes.

'Is this your home?' I ask.

Mercy shakes her head. 'Wait here,' she says, slipping off Lady, walking past the house and disappearing into a dense thicket. I sit on Lady and wait.

And wait.

I start to eat the last of the stolen quinces to pass the time.

'Mercy?' I say, not quite shouting.

Silence.

While I wait, I tie Lady to the fence, slowly push the front door open and peer into the house. There's an upturned table and two broken chairs, puddles of rainwater on the floor and pigeons sitting on the rafters, persistently cooing. It's even less inviting than a damp forest floor.

Someone taps me on my shoulder from behind and I am so lost in thought that I stumble backwards, into Mercy's arms.

'It's only me!' she says, laughing and giving me a hug. 'You shouldn't really be in here, the roof could collapse at any time. Come with me.'

I follow her outside, my face burning with embarrassment for being as skittish as Lady in the eerie forest, but secretly feeling pleased that Mercy's initial anger has been replaced by affection. I watch as she unties Lady and absently kisses her neck, and then walk closely behind as she leads my horse around the thicket to a small clearing where the early evening sun is streaming through the trees. She ties Lady up next to another horse, its dark chestnut coat flecked with white. A red roan, just like Thomas's horse.

She sees me staring. 'Oh, that's Plum. I named her when I was nine, because of the redness of her coat in the sun. She will be glad of some company.'

'She is beautiful!' I exclaim.

The two horses look at each other, prick their ears and make soft whinnying sounds.

Animals find it so much easier to be friends than we do.

'Welcome to my home,' Mercy says, pride creeping into her voice. 'I built a fire to help us dry off.' She carefully places a log on the fire and it bursts into life.

Just beyond the horses is a shelter made of intertwined branches and leaves and moss, woven tightly together to keep gusts of wind from blowing in. 'Did you build this?' I ask. She nods as if it's obvious that she could build something so elaborate. 'It's exquisite, Mercy.'

Clusters of herbs hang, suspended on string tied between the shelter and a sapling, and catch the dappled sunlight.

'I will warm up some acorns and nettles,' says Mercy, hanging a blackened pan above the fire, before sitting cross-legged as close as she dares to the flames.

'Thank you,' I say, sitting down opposite her and warming my hands in front of the fire. I'm shivering again and my eyes feel heavy; I could sleep for a thousand years. 'Let's eat the rest of the cheese and bread that I stole from the market while we wait.'

We sit in silence, eating greedily and staring at the orange flames dancing around the crackling wood.

'Mercy,' I say finally. 'Why do you live here alone? You

are so young! Why was the Witchfinder General trying to drown you? What did you do?'

She stirs the pot, but doesn't respond.

I swallow hard. 'I am sorry. I didn't mean to ask what *you* did wrong. I wanted to know what *he* thought you'd done.'

Her face softens. 'I understand. I am thirteen – not so young.'

'You are a year older than me!'

She clears her throat. 'Listen carefully as I will only tell you this story once. Even before the war, my family was poor. We were nothing. The kind of family that is invisible to others. Father died long ago and Mother earned money by making remedies for wounded soldiers, so that she could provide for me and my five siblings. Most of the soldiers survived. But the villagers heard that they could make money by denouncing women as witches, so they told the Witchfinder General's men that Mother was a witch making magic potions. They betrayed my mother's kindness.'

Shivers travel up my spine.

'My mother was – *is* – a herbalist too.'

The flames reflect in Mercy's eyes as she looks at me across the fire. 'Well, then, you understand more than most.'

'But why was it you on the bridge, rather than your mother?' I ask gently.

'I couldn't let her die. She has to care for my sisters and brother,' Mercy says, staring into the fire. 'So I confessed to making the remedies – or potions, as the soldiers insist on calling them – and then I ran away from home, planning to return when the war against witches was over. Mother taught us how to eat by foraging in the fields and forest for food, but I wanted to leave a hidden note for my cousin in Dedham, to tell my family I'm well.'

She looks down at her hands and pulls at the rough

skin around her nails. 'I assumed the Witchfinder General would be distracted by the women he is trying to capture, but one of his men recognised me. I only got as far as the village square. I was foolish to go on market day.'

'No,' I say. 'You were thinking of your family. It was just bad luck that you were seen.'

Mercy shrugs, her eyes glistening. 'Maybe.'

She separates the soup into two bowls and we eat as the sky darkens.

'Aye, it was a busy market day and you could easily have gone unnoticed.'

'Your accent is strange. Unfamiliar.'

I smile. 'So is yours. I am Scottish.'

Mercy frowns. 'Why did you come to Essex all the way from Scotland?'

'I came here to find ...'

'Your mother?'

I nod.

My chest tightens. 'The Witchfinder General's men took her.'

'I am not surprised. I've heard that the dungeon in his castle is full of women who have done nothing but show compassion to others.' She pokes angrily at the fire with a stick. 'I fear for them. It's not so long until the summer solstice hangings.'

'You know about the hangings?'

'*Everyone* around here knows,' she says, poking at the fire so hard that sparks fly up into the night air. 'I wish I could find a way to stop that evil man in his castle of death. I was thinking of joining the Inseparables, but they talk too much and I am probably too young anyway.'

'Who are the Inseparables?'

'A group of girls, a few years older than us, whose mothers were killed by the Witchfinder General. They always appear as three, but hardly anyone knows how many of them there are because they wear black cloaks with the hoods up so their faces can't be seen.'

The figures on the bridge!

'The cloaked figures are girls?'

Mercy nods. 'Why are you smiling?'

'I think those girls saved our lives on the bridge by creating a distraction.'

'They might have helped, but *you* saved *my* life,' says Mercy quietly. 'Twice, in fact. In the water and again when that man appeared out of nowhere holding a sword. I still can't believe you saved me.'

The magnitude of the day's events hits me at once. I try to focus on the fire, but it's a blur. I can no longer see Mercy. Her hands are under my arms, pulling me up, her strength surprising, the shelter warm, the woollen blanket heavy. I hear Mercy talking to Lady in a soothing voice, telling her that she is safe here, that no one can hurt us now.

14

18 June 1647

Three days to summer solstice

I am falling into never-ending blackness. My arms and legs thrash around as I fall past my silent father, past my beloved brother, his face hot with fever. I am underwater and there is Cecily gasping for air, but I cannot reach her. I am running through a vast forest towards Malkin as she tries to claw her way out of the cloth bag. Sweet Malkin, I am here! Four kittens lift from the earth and float away.

Three days left.

I sit up, rubbing my eyes.

I look out of the makeshift window on one side of the

shelter. The fire is lit, but there is no sign of Mercy.

'Mercy?'

There is no reply. She has left me: I can feel it in my bones. Cecily disowned me and now Mercy has gone too.

'Art! Why are you crying? Did you have a bad dream?' Mercy rushes into the shelter and sits down beside me, her arm around my shoulders.

I stiffen at her touch. 'I thought you'd gone.'

'I had,' she says cheerfully. 'I was checking the horses. Come here.'

She pulls me towards her. I try and push her away, but eventually I give in and collapse into her as hot, salty tears run down my face and drip on to her arm. I expect her to squirm, but instead she holds me even closer.

You will meet your guides along the way – be open to them. How did Mother know?

Eventually Mercy loosens her arms from our embrace. 'Come and sit by the fire,' she says. 'I made you a remedy that Mother calls "fortifying". You need some help to regain your strength.'

'Thank you,' I say, standing up and following her outside, my throat as dry as dust. The dress she was wearing yesterday is drying out on the branch of a tree, next to my coat; today she is wearing a shirt with the cuffs rolled up tightly and a pair of trousers cut off at the bottom, a sword tucked into her belt. The clothes, which I assume belong to her brother, are much more suitable than that flimsy dress, I think to myself, sitting by the fire and slowly sipping the sour, bitter drink from the bowl, feeling its heat warm my body.

'The taste is familiar,' I say. 'Is the sourness from purslane?'

'I'm not sure. I know that rye is good for aching heads and wood sage eases sweats – you were so hot

Purslane

in the night I feared fever would take you. But I can't remember why purslane is good, I just know my mother always uses it.'

'Wait a moment,' I say, standing up and reaching into the inside pocket of my coat. 'My mother gave me her recipe book.'

Mercy and I sit shoulder to shoulder, turning the pages slowly.

'Your mother's drawings are incredible,' says Mercy, her fingers tracing the delicate violet flowers of the periwinkle. 'You must be so pleased to have this special book.'

'Yes,' I say, nodding. 'But also worried about losing it … here it is! Purslane: a herb of the moon. It cools and eases nightmares. You were absolutely right.'

'Of course! I also added hawthorn seed, bruised and boiled in water, for inward tormenting pains, because I think your heart was broken when your mother was taken.'

I cannot look at Mercy for fear of more tears falling. I am so grateful she understands; I don't think I could find the words to explain.

'You are very kind, Mercy,' I say.

'It's easy being kind to the girl who saved my life,' says Mercy. 'Now, let us assume your mother is alive. If the Witchfinder's men took her, she will be in the dungeon of his castle. How will you get into the dungeon? Is the plan to pretend to be a witch so that you will be thrown inside with all the other women? If so, you will have to find a way of looking like a girl again. And even then, you might well end up being killed.'

You will not be able to rescue your mother alone. You will not have to.

I want to repeat Maude's words, but I suddenly realise how stupid I might sound. A woman appeared out of nowhere, gave me advice and an amulet and disappeared.

The answer to your dilemma is to be found among the horses.

153

'I thought I could perhaps get a job as a stable boy at the castle,' I say slowly, finally starting to understand Maude's guiding words. 'And then … work out a way rescue Mother.' I look at the ground, embarrassed. 'Other than that, I haven't got a proper plan yet.'

Mercy laughs, but not unkindly. 'Perhaps you had to imagine you could find your mother easily because otherwise you would never have left Scotland.'

'I would have left anyway,' I say. 'I wasn't welcome there. It was no longer my home.'

'It is the same for both of us; my home is no longer home either. But it won't be easy to get into the castle nor to stop the Witchfinder; both are well protected by guards.'

'He might be protected by guards, but he is not protected from us, Mercy.' I jump to my feet, laughing and slicing the air with my knife. 'The Witchfinder is not immortal!'

Mercy is on her feet too. 'And if he is not immortal then he is not invincible. And if he's not invincible then we can …'

'Poison him with potions!'

I pick up Mother's recipe book and turn to the pages at the back. 'Dangerous herbs, to be avoided at all costs: water hemlock; deadly nightshade; white snakeroot. That should do it!'

Mercy's face is flushed. 'Let us poison all his guards and then poison him!' she says, hopping from one foot to the other. 'We can poison everyone who supports him, who fails to speak up against him and who tries to silence women!'

I sit back down. 'That would make us as bad as the Witchfinder and his men,' I say quietly. 'I don't believe in an eye for an eye. There has to be another way.'

Mercy stands still and looks down at me, disappointment shadowing her face. 'I thought you wanted to save your mother?' she asks, leaning back against the thick trunk of an elm tree, her hands thrust inside her pockets.

'Perhaps your idea of becoming a stable boy is not so bad after all,' she adds, sliding down the trunk to sit awkwardly on the twisted knot of tree roots. 'We could both try and become stable boys.'

'You would do that for me?'

'Well, you cannot do it on your own,' she says.

I run my hand through my short, spiky hair and look at her long blonde hair. 'If you are serious and you want to help me, then there's something we have to do.'

*

Mercy bends over and her hair almost touches the ground. Neither of us has a pair of scissors, so I use a blunt knife. I take a handful of her hair and slowly start hacking.

'Stop!' Mercy jumps away from me. 'Are we making a mistake? Are you sure this is the right thing to do? I am not sure I want to look like a boy.'

'Yesterday you nearly drowned because you are a girl. We have no chance of getting into the castle if we don't look like real stable boys. Besides, your hair will grow back in time.'

I dig deep into my pocket and pull out the lock of my hair, a reminder of my old self, even though, somehow, I feel more myself than before. 'You could keep a lock of your hair too?'

'Cut it before I change my mind,' she says, bending over and clasping her hands behind her back.

When I have finished, she carefully puts a lock in her pocket before she gathers up fistfuls of old hair and throws it on the fire, watching silently as the flames burst upwards. The acrid smell is so strong that we both turn away.

'There is one more thing,' I say,

speaking loudly over the crackling fire. 'If we are to be boys, we need boys' names. I know you said Art is an odd name for a boy, but my name can be for a girl *or* a boy. It might help if you had a name that starts with "M" so that it sounds familiar to you. I was thinking of "Mack". It was my great-grandfather's name. It means "son of". What do you think?'

She cocks her head to one side. 'Mack. Mercy. Mack. Do you think it suits me?'

'Yes,' I say. 'It's preferable to Cuthbert or Bartholomew. Or Humphrey.'

Mercy laughs. 'It would be an honour to borrow your great-grandfather's name. Thank you. Now let's go and collect some herbs.'

*

I follow Mercy along the burn. She

Nettles

is quick and nimble, bending down every now and again, picking flowers and leaves, or using her sword to cut nettles and placing them inside her cloth bag. After the long days alone with Lady, I want to keep talking, but Mercy seems happy to walk in silence.

Finally, she stops at a pond decorated with yellow lilies that contrast brightly against the reflection of the perfectly blue sky.

'I wanted to look at my hair in the reflection, but now I feel vain and silly. What if I don't like what I see?' Mercy asks.

'We could look together,' I suggest. Mercy smiles and I reach for her hand.

We stand by the edge of the pond and lean as far forward as we dare. I see that our reflections are simply another version of ourselves, distorted and ever changing.

'You are going to fall in!' I say, pulling Mercy back from the edge of the water. 'You don't have to tilt that far over to see yourself. Let's stand here, where there aren't so many lilies.'

Mercy stares at herself, pulling at the tufts of her hair. 'I'm light-headed. I'm not quite myself, but I like the way I feel.'

'Let's go back,' I say. 'I want to show you something.'

I take the two coils of rope from the bottom of the saddlebag and within no time, the shorter one is stretched taut between two trees, several feet above the ground. I tear the leaves off a fallen branch, remove my boots, hold on to the tree trunk and pull myself efficiently on to the rope. Mercy stops hanging the herbs to dry and looks up at me, her eyes wide. Holding the branch as a balancing pole, I step delicately on to the rope. It's rough underneath my bare feet, coarse enough to burn and blister the skin, but I try to not let it distract me as I move forward.

'One. Two. Three. Four. Damn!' I tumble to the ground. I try again. Still I fall.

I will never be as good as Thomas. How disappointed he would be if he could see me now! He believed in me, but I don't believe in myself.

I take a deep breath.

I will prove to myself that I can do this. Not for Thomas, but for me.

I start again. This time, I will practise balancing first. I lean the branch against the tree, stand on the rope again and balance for as long as I possibly can on one foot, putting my arm out to touch the tree when I start to sway. I step away from the tree, waving my arms, then holding them out straight. I swap feet. It is always easier to balance on my right foot. I turn around and lean lightly against the tree again. This time, I focus my gaze on the tree on the other side. I start to sway, but I wave my arms to balance myself.

Now I must try again, with the branch to guide me. My arms are spread out. The branch must never drop lower than my armpits. My body must not tip forward nor backwards. I take another deep breath and feel a sense of calm wash through my body. I move forward quickly and gracefully. I am almost at the end, just a couple more steps to go …

Thomas would be proud. I am proud of myself.

'Art! That's amazing. Can you teach me? Maybe we can tightrope walk into the Witchfinder's castle!'

I tumble to the ground, landing on my bottom with a thud.

'Oh, Art, I'm sorry,' Mercy says, pulling me up.

'Don't worry. It happens all the time,' I say, laughing and brushing dry leaves off my legs. 'Would you like me to teach you? Take your boots off. Put both feet on the rope and stand facing the tree. Try to balance, but hold on to the tree trunk if you need to … That's it!'

Mercy stands on the rope, sways and tumbles to the ground.

'Try not to be so tense. Don't look at your feet. Focus on the tree in front of you. Put your arms out wide and use them to balance. Keep your back straight. Yes, that's it! Now, turn around and try to take a few steps.'

'One. Two. Three,' says Mercy, before falling off the rope, straight on to her feet this time. She gets up and stands on the rope again. 'One. Two. Three. Four. Five. Six.' She keeps going. I watch in disbelief; it took me weeks of practice to get halfway across the rope and Mercy has done it straight away.

'You're a natural!'

'I used to have this competition with my brother when we were young,' Mercy says, pulling her boots back on, her face bursting into a smile. 'We would climb old trees and walk out on to the thickest branches. It was a stupid, dangerous thing to do and we stopped when my brother fell and injured his arm. Mother made a remedy that eased the pain and eventually his arm healed, but she made us promise not to do it again. It was worth it, though!'

I slide my sword from its sheath. 'If we are to enter the Witchfinder's castle, we have to be excellent at sword fighting too. Shall we?' I place both feet firmly on the ground and tip my chest forward. Mercy takes her sword out with a flourish and I twist and turn to avoid her, groaning as I lunge towards her, my hand movements becoming faster as my sword clashes noisily against hers, beads of sweat forming on my forehead and sliding down my face. I am careful not to touch her, but Mercy looks tired and although I could keep going and going, I slow down.

'You are strong,' says Mercy, gasping for air. 'I would not care to have you as my opponent in a fight.'

The heat travels up my neck, to my cheeks.

I must learn to take a compliment!

I flop to the ground and look up at the blue sky, which is streaked with wisps of white clouds. Mercy lies down next to me, still breathing heavily, her shoulder next to mine.

'Who taught you to fight so well, Art?'

'My brother.'

'Where is he now?'

I swallow. 'He's dead. Typhus.'

'I'm so sorry,' she says. 'Do you have a sister?'

I don't want to tell her that Mary died before her life started. I don't want her to know how alone I am in this world. Not just yet.

'No,' I say.

'Do you miss Scotland?'

'I …' I cannot speak.

'Of course you do,' she says. 'That was a silly question. I will think of another. Do you believe in magic?'

'I believe in nature, in animals and trees and the

seasons. I believe in black cats and owls and foxes. I believe in kindness.'

'I believe in you, Art,' says Mercy.

'You said that you'd do anything for me.'

'And I meant it. I will help you to find your mother.'

'I was going to ask you to promise not to turn your back on me.' I pause. 'I had a best friend once but she betrayed me.'

'I promise,' says Mercy as we look up at the clouds passing slowly above us. I notice one drifting into the shape of a cat with a long tail. I turn to Mercy to ask her if she can see it too, but she is fast asleep, her mouth slightly open. 'Hello, Malkin,' I whisper, as I fall into a dreamless sleep.

15

19 June 1647

Two days to summer solstice

According to Mother's recipe book, the archangel is a woman's herb often referred to as a 'herb of Venus', but more commonly known by the name of 'dead nettle'. Only the flowers are of use; the plants with white flowers bend downwards while those with red flowers push up through hedges, but it is the yellow archangels that flourish in the dampness of woods that I am harvesting.

I empty the pale yellow flowers into my pan with some water from the burn and show Mercy. 'I thought we should be prepared for any injury.'

She nods. 'Good to bring forth splinters and calm bruises.'

I put the pan on the fire and stir the yellow flowers with a clean stick. 'Also, to stop nose bleeds. And heal wounds.'

Mercy laughs. 'We sound very serious, like physicians.'

'Aye. Or, if you are foolish enough not to believe in herbal remedies, a pair of blood-sucking witches with a herd of invisible familiars.'

Oh, how I miss Malkin!

'If you and I are witches because our mothers heal people, then so be it,' says Mercy. 'I would rather be a witch than a witchfinder. It is a very good idea to be prepared.'

She lays a piece of oak bark on a stone and bashes it again and again with a stone. She works steadily, until the bark turns into a pulp, scrapes the pulp into a bowl, fills it with water and sits it in direct sunlight. She wipes the stone clean and carefully places a small plant on it that has a single, blueish-green leaf with sweet-smelling white flowers and tiny berries.

'I know that oak bark can be applied directly to a wound to aid healing, but I have never seen that plant before,' I say.

'It's called the "one blade" because of its single leaf,' says Mercy. 'It dies very quickly after the berries appear. Mother says it is one of the most precious herbs because, mixed with equal parts wine and vinegar, it is a remedy for those infected with the plague. But it's also the best plant to apply to wounds, both old and new, without having anything added to it.'

'I know we were jesting before, but do you think we are at great risk of being injured?' I ask.

'We are taking a great risk simply by attempting to enter the castle,' says Mercy, gently crushing the plant's single leaf and red berries.

She hits the root of the plant hard and Lady jumps.

'Sssssshhhh, Lady,' I say. 'It's just Mercy preparing a remedy.'

A bellowing of bullfinches, their chests a blur of red, rises out of a hawthorn bush.

Mercy turns to look at me and her mouth falls open. I freeze and slowly follow her gaze. A boy on a large grey

horse, staring down at us. I notice the sunlight catching his eyes. Green with a ring of gold around each pupil.

We didn't hear him because Mercy was making so much noise. We forgot we were outlaws. We will surely be dead before dusk falls. Breathe. Slowly. Deeply. One. Two ...

The boy dismounts.

I jump to my feet, hand on my sword.

Mercy stands in front of the stone and wipes her hands on her trousers.

'What are you doing here?' he says finally, in a threatening tone.

'Hunting for pheasants and foraging, sir,' says Mercy.

Sir! He is a year older than Mercy at the very most. I think again. She is not taking any risks.

'Why do you have so many herbs hanging out to dry?' he asks. 'And why were you hitting that stone so hard?'

Mercy points at the stone. 'Oh, that. We're making

171

marinades for the pheasant meat, sir. As I'm sure you know, it can be very dry and Father prefers it with some additional flavour.'

'And who are you?' I ask. Mercy frowns at me and shakes her head. I start again. 'Sorry. Would you like some water, sir?'

'Thank you,' he says, taking the bowl and drinking it all at once. 'You boys are too young to be out here alone. What are your names?'

'I am Art and this is my brother Mack,' I say. 'And your name, sir?'

'Elijah Wolf,' he says. 'I don't suppose you have seen the Inseparables? A group of three who wear black cloaks with the hoods pulled up to cover their faces. I have been looking for them for days.'

A wave of nausea washes through my body. *This boy is probably looking for them after the incident on the bridge. What if he recognises Mercy, despite her disguise?*

172

'I don't know anyone going by that name, sir,' says Mercy.

'Well,' he continues, 'if you do see them, do not approach them. They might well use their magic potions to put a wicked spell on you.'

'That sounds hideous. We understand,' says Mercy, nodding.

Elijah turns his attention back to me. 'I assume you are the oldest, Art. Are you able to look after your brother until your father returns?'

'Yes, most definitely, sir,' I say, holding the hilt of my sword tight and tracing the engravings with my fingers to calm myself.

'With the Inseparables running free, you need to have your wits about you.' He drops his horse's reins. 'Perhaps a friendly duel is in order to ensure you do.'

A duel? My heart quickens.

'My brother is a very strong fighter,' says Mercy,

looking at me, her eyebrows raised in encouragement.

Elijah and I pull our swords out at the same time. I grip mine tight with both hands. We stand opposite each other, our swords raised.

It's no different to fighting Thomas.

Elijah steps forward. He is a little taller than me and quick as well as strong. As he cuts across my body, I step back. He swipes at me and I lift the blade. I push his sword out of the way. We dance backwards and forwards. Our swords collide and clash.

'Your brother is right,' he says, out of breath, but not yet defeated. 'You *are* strong.'

'Thank you,' I say, looking over at Mercy. My concentration lapses and the tip of his sword catches my lower arm. I drop my sword and grasp my bloody arm. It stings, and I bite my lip hard to stop the tears.

'That wasn't very friendly, sir,' says Mercy, coming closer.

'I am sorry, Art,' says Elijah. 'I didn't mean to …'

'You should go now,' says Mercy, her voice firm. 'You have hurt my brother. Please leave.'

Elijah mounts his horse and rides into the sun-dappled forest.

'Don't forget,' he shouts over his shoulder. 'If you see the Inseparables, find a soldier as soon as you can and alert him.'

*

'I don't trust that boy. We have to leave soon,' Mercy says, taking the archangel flowers out of the pan, dabbing them dry and tipping the remaining water on to the stone to clear away the remains of the poultice. She stamps furiously on the dying embers of the fire and kicks earth over it.

The oak bark stings the cut on my right arm, but I press it down hard and try not to grimace. 'Thank you for healing me,' I say. 'I will call you "Magic Mack" from now on.'

Mercy points to my arm. 'You don't have to stand there for ever, holding on to your arm as though it might fall off. The poultice will dry and crumble once it has done its work. Here, pack your blanket.'

I take the blanket. 'Shall I help you dismantle the shelter? We could perhaps take some of the moss with us as it's dried out.'

'Don't worry. My cousin told me that the Inseparables have built more than half a dozen shelters across this stretch of Essex. We will recognise them because they always leave the same sign: a collection of stones in ever decreasing circles. And there are many more built by other foragers that we are free to use.'

Relief washes over me. 'Is there one close to the castle?'

'Yes, there are shelters all over Essex. I am sure we can find a suitable one.'

We mount our horses and I follow Mercy as Plum

weaves delicately in and out of the trees. It is safer not to talk. We come to the edge of the forest, where the long grass bends in the warm breeze and bumblebees hum in and out of foxgloves, giddy on pollen. A small herd of deer look up at us with passing curiosity. Wildflowers crowd together, their bright colours vying for attention. The bright magenta of the corncockle. The pale pink of the cuckoo flower. The vivid blue of the cornflower. Blood red poppies next to the delicate pink midsummer orchids.

My heart lurches.

Midsummer.

'Mercy,' I say, my voice cracking. 'It's only two days till solstice.'

'I know,' she says. 'We will no doubt be able to find a shelter close to the castle, but we cannot risk Elijah Wolf finding us again. We might have to ride inland, back towards Dedham.'

'I can't ride in the opposite direction from Manningtree,' I say quietly. *Two days.* Tears prick my eyes. I take a deep breath. 'Before you go, can you show me where the castle is, so that I don't waste time trying to find it?'

Mercy stops Plum and they both stare at me. 'What do you intend to do? Ride up to the portcullis and demand the Witchfinder liberate your mother?'

'Please just tell me where the castle is and Lady and I shall be on our way.'

'No,' she says, sighing. 'I won't tell you. Nor shall I leave you. Since leaving home I have been very careful. But I am no longer alone. I have you. I said I would do anything for you and I shall not let you down, Art. It might be safer to build our own shelter near to the castle in case the Witchfinder's men have discovered the hidden shelters and are spying on them. I don't want to take any risks.' She smiles. 'But if we can find a fallen tree and a large enough dry spot, I can show you how to build a secret shelter. You are my best friend, Art Flynt. You can't get rid of me so easily.'

I nod. If I try to speak, I know I will cry.

*

We stand by the ancient oak as our horses tear up tufts of grass. The tree lies on the forest floor like a fallen soldier, still commanding in death.

Mercy runs a hand along the rough bark. 'It's perfect. It was probably blown over in a storm last winter and isn't yet rotten. We need to collect two dozen long, sturdy branches and lean them against this side of the tree, which will protect us from the wind. Fallen branches with leaves still on them are best as they offer more protection. We can build a fire pit on the other side. It's perfectly dry here, so we shouldn't be too damp at night.'

We build the shelter quickly and Mercy digs a shallow hole in the ground with her hands while I collect kindling and the driest sticks I can find.

'We have plenty of herbs for supper, but I shall have to forage for nettles, beechnuts and hawthorn,' says Mercy, wiping the earth off her hands with a dock leaf. 'It won't get dark for a while as it's so close to the longest day … sorry, Art. You hardly need to be reminded.'

Dock leaves

'Why don't I look for a burn to refill the flasks with water?' I ask. 'I doubt I'll have to go too far.'

'That sounds like a good plan,' Mercy says, bending to examine a pale mushroom sprouting from the bottom of a nearby tree. 'Keep your cap pulled down and don't ride east because you will eventually arrive at the castle. I would like to see you again.'

I'd like to see you again too.

16

The air in the forest is warm and still. Lady canters along the wide pathways until we reach a burn and she pulls up; she always seems to sense when I am breathless from riding too fast.

'Thank you for stopping, Lady,' I say, as I dismount and kneel by the edge of the water. I watch as a great egret wades slowly on its long, thin black legs, its wings pulled in tight to its body, its S-shaped neck stretched forward. It plunges its sharp yellow beak into the water, lifts out a small frog, swallows it whole and strides away.

Nature is so beautiful, yet often so cruel.

I cup the cool, refreshing water in my hands and splash my face. Three summers ago, it was so unusually sunny in Kelso that Cecily and I were able to slip off the chalky riverbank and float on our backs in the black water for minutes at a time. We lay there, arms and legs outstretched, staring silently at the clear blue sky.

I stand up in a daze. I left Kelso six days ago. Six days since I sat at the back of the church and listened to the minister taunting his parishioners about witches and potions and the devil and *my* mother. I clench my fists. I hear his triumphant voice. *Agnes Flynt has a third nipple! She has a birthmark on her back* ... I swallow hard.

I hear Mother's voice. *Do not be afraid to take risks.*

Lady looks at me, unblinking. 'I feel better now, Lady.' I mount her, take a long, deep breath and turn east, just as Mercy told us not to do.

*

Scottish castles are often as grey as the skies above them, but this one is different. It is magnificent. Perhaps it's because the evening sky is streaked red, but this castle seems to almost be aflame, the bricks a burned orange colour that is magnified in the vast moat surrounding it. Pulling back branches, I count six, seven, eight turrets before giving up. Hidden in a thicket of trees on a small hill, I am too far away to even begin to count the arrow slits.

'Lady,' I say. 'How will we ever enter *that* castle?'

She paws the ground. 'Yes, I am afraid too, Lady.'

I have barely talked to her for days and I suddenly realise how much I have missed it. 'We don't have any explosives to weaken the walls,' I say, my voice dropping to a whisper again. 'We cannot enter through the main entrance. No doubt there will be a murder hole above the portcullis. Do you know what that is, Lady?'

She snorts. 'This is a serious matter. You *must* know

what a murder hole is. You are an educated horse. I am sure Mother told me and Thomas all about castles while I was grooming you.'

I mount Lady again and she holds her head high, her ears forward, her eyes bright. Talking to her soothes my nerves. It gives me courage.

I am so close to Mother. And yet ... I may not reach her in time.

I am pretending that I am fine, talking balderdash to Lady to protect myself, but I am not. Mother is in the castle with its burned orange bricks and crenelated walls and a sparkling moat to distract people from the atrocities taking place inside, and I am here, hiding behind trees, watching the sky slowly darken and deceiving Mercy.

I have to be positive.

'What was I saying? Oh, yes. A murder hole is a small opening in the ceiling. For dropping rocks, boiling water or hot oil on enemies.'

A wedge of geese flies overhead in a perfect

V-formation, honking loudly. Lady tenses. I stroke her neck. Her ears flatten against her head.

'Lady,' I whisper. 'What's wrong?'

A loud crack echoes through the trees. Lady rears up. I loosen the reins so that she doesn't lose balance and lean my upper body towards her neck.

The musket fires again. It's closer this time.

Why did I take such a huge risk? Why did I come here?

I dare not lift my head and look around.

My mouth is dry. I cannot swallow. When I was in the attic alone, Mother told me to count backwards from a hundred.

I say the numbers in my head, as slowly as I can.

100. 99. 98. 97. 96. 95.

I squeeze my eyes shut.

94. 93. 92. 91.

Lady rears up again and it is all I can do to stay on her back.

90. 89.

'Follow me,' says a voice so softly that I am sure I imagined it.

I open my eyes. The boy is there, in front of me, on his horse.

'Elijah?'

He puts a finger on his lips and then points to his left.

Don't trust that boy.

I don't move.

His eyes widen. 'You have to follow me,' he whispers. 'Or they will mistake you for an Inseparable in the dusk light and shoot you.'

Elijah turns his horse to the left and trots down a narrow, overgrown pathway that I hadn't noticed. I don't know where he might take me and Mercy will be desperately worried, but I have no choice. I sit upright and follow him.

*

Elijah doesn't turn around. He doesn't say a word. As we ride deeper into the woods, the musket shots become muffled and more distant, until we can't hear them at all.

Finally, Elijah stops and turns, his face illuminated by the waxing moon.

It is later than I thought! How long have I been away from the camp?

His horse is almost muzzle to muzzle with Lady. I move her backwards slightly, creating more space between us.

'You are good with horses,' says Elijah. 'You know how to control him. You even stayed on him when the musket fired and he reared up.'

'She.'

'He, she, what does it matter? I was impressed.'

He looks at me, as though waiting for me to thank him. I say nothing. I won't give him the satisfaction.

'Anyway, what were you doing in the forest alone?' he asks. 'It's dangerous. And why were you looking at the castle?'

'I got lost,' I say.

Completely lost.

'Sometimes I too am lost,' he says, looking at the ground. 'Sometimes I don't want to be me.'

'Now you are talking in riddles. What were *you* doing in the forest?'

'I was with the men who were shooting muskets. They were teasing me; they are older than me and they can be merciless.'

If he was with the men shooting muskets, he must be equally cruel and heartless.

I take a deep breath.

Can he hear my heart thumping?

'I'm sure they mean well,' I say, trying my best to sound sincere. 'Thank you for guiding me to safety, but I really ought to be on my way. Mack will be waiting.'

'You are lost. I will take you back to your new camp.'

My blood runs cold. *He knows.*

Think quickly.

If I accidentally ride east again in the dark, I might well encounter the men with the muskets and this time I might not be so lucky. I have to face the truth. I am lost. I also need to keep up appearances – if Elijah believes that Mercy and I are foragers, we have nothing to hide.

I shrug and try to sound as indifferent as I can. 'Show me the way.'

*

The path is wide and Elijah rides just ahead of me without talking, but the silence isn't easy like it is with Mercy. I try to think of something to say without giving anything away.

'You said the men with the muskets can be merciless.'

'Indeed. I don't want you to judge me,' he says, looking straight ahead. 'Boys can be cruel.'

'I'm not … one of those boys.'

'I know. I wouldn't be talking to you like this if I

thought you were like them. It's my mother. They tease me about her.'

I wait for him to continue, but he rides on in silence.

My mind races.

Is she locked up with my mother? Impossible. Is she a herbalist too? Also impossible – why would he be working with the Witchfinder's soldiers?

Eventually, I cannot stop myself from prompting him and I say gently, 'You mentioned your mother.'

He slows his horse down so that it can walk alongside Lady. 'She was the daughter of a Moorish trader, originally from North Africa. She was born in London and met my father, a sea captain, when they were both young.' He talks quickly, the words tumbling steadily out of his mouth. 'They married and almost immediately Mother fell pregnant with me. Shortly afterwards, my father went away to sea and never came back. Mother was heartbroken. A few years later, she heard from another sea captain that my father was seen in Portugal, so she saved up all the money she could and went to find him.'

'And what happened to you when she was away?'

'My mother's sister looked after me. But, with six children of her own, she didn't really want me.'

Aunt Elizabeth with her mouth set in a thin, mean line. Elijah's aunt, being left with an unwanted child.

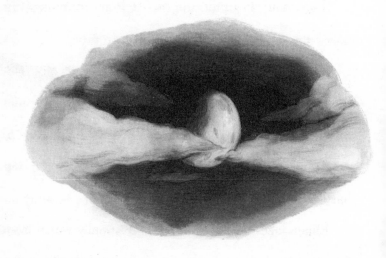

A cloud passes over the moon and a few huge raindrops fall from the sky.

Elijah sighs. 'I am feeling sorry for myself at the moment. Among other things, I run the stables in the castle and one of the head boys broke his leg falling off a stallion a few days ago. The Witchfinder must not find out that we are a man down; soldiers are nothing without their horses and, as you know, horses have to be exercised and well cared for.'

'I love horses,' I blurt out before I can stop myself. 'I could help in the stables?'

Elijah, lost in thought, doesn't reply and my face flushes with shame.

What was I thinking?

'I should return to camp before the storm,' I say hastily.

Elijah gazes up at the sky. 'It's unusually warm even for a summer's night, but the storm won't come for a day or two.'

Summer solstice.

He turns to look at me. 'You are terribly pale. I don't think it's just the moonlight. You need to rest. If you ride straight on and then take the next path on the left, you will know where you are. I'm sure Mack will be waiting for you.'

If he knows exactly where we set up camp, he must have been spying on us!

He wipes the raindrops off his face and turns his horse around. 'I will see you again very soon.'

He is gone before I can reply.

*

I tie Lady up and sit next to Mercy by the fire. 'I ate without you,' she says, not looking up. 'But I saved some for you. It's in the bowl over there.'

I barely taste the crushed nettles and nuts. I just want to eat and sleep, but I know I have to be honest with Mercy first. 'I saw the castle,' I say hesitantly.

Mercy pokes at the fire and red embers colour the

night air. She clenches her jaw. 'Did anyone see you?'

'No. Well, yes. I saw Elijah. I know you don't think he can be trusted. But what choice do I have? It's two days until summer solstice. I have to find a way of entering the castle tomorrow.'

Mercy frowns, deep in thought. 'It's been a very long day. Let's sleep now and talk again at dawn.'

I lie in the shelter on a bed of leaves and watch the last of the fire flicker. I don't expect sleep to come, but as soon as I shut my eyes I fall into darkness.

17

20 June 1647

One day to summer solstice

Candles flicker, their warm light illuminating the tunnel and casting long shadows on the old stone walls. The women are weak. They cannot move. The stench! I shine the candle in the face of every woman I pass. There are hundreds of women. I cannot see where the dungeon ends. One woman with wild hair and a pale face lifts her head to look at the candle. Mother! I drop to my knees to embrace her, but my arms go straight through her body. She pulls a hood over her head and her face fades away. I reach out again, but the black cloak falls silently to the floor. Mother is no more.

Mercy is holding me down, her hand over my

mouth. 'Sorry to have to wake you up like this, but you were screaming "Mother" and we can't draw attention to ourselves.' She looks down at me, her face full of tenderness and concern.

'We will find her,' she says. 'I promise.'

I pull myself free and sit up and calm myself by focusing on the small but perfect spheres of dew that cling to the long grass outside the shelter and the birds embracing the new day in vibrant song.

'I am fine now,' I say.

Mercy walks around nearby trees, hands interlaced behind her back, looking at the ground. She examines a prickly green plant with dark green oak-shaped leaves and pale pink flowers that push up towards the light, crouches down and pinches its delicate stems between her thumb and forefinger.

'As I'm sure you know, this is motherwort,' she says, waving it in the air. 'Mother's herb. A herb of the heart. It will ease your anguish.'

She boils the dark green leaves in the pan until they wilt, then passes me a steaming cup. The tea is almost too bitter to swallow, but its effect is magical: my breath is less shallow, my heart slows down, the fear subsides.

'Thank you, Mercy,' I say. 'Why don't we walk the rope again? Whenever I was upset in Kelso, my brother would remind me that rope practice is good not only for balance and strength, but also for courage and fearlessness.'

I take the long rope from the saddlebag, find a long branch and strip it of its leaves. I remove my boots, tie the rope high up between two medium-sized tree trunks, ensure that it's taut and climb one of the trees.

'I shall climb the other,' says Mercy, moving up through the branches of the tree quickly. 'I'd rather encourage you from up here.'

I have never walked this high and it's reassuring to see her there, at the other end of the rope. Before stepping

out, I find my equilibrium, shutting my eyes and allowing myself a moment just to be. I pull the moonstone amulet from beneath my shirt, hold it in the palm of my hand and recall Maude's words: *Do not grieve for that which has yet to come to pass.*

There is still time to rescue Mother. I have to find a way.

I hold the branch out in front of me and allow my bare feet to guide me. One step. Two. Three. My body feels light, my breath soft. Four. Five. Six. The rope is coarse beneath my feet. I am halfway there. I shouldn't look down, but I do. I glance at Lady intuitively, expecting to see her dozing or grazing. Instead her tail is swishing furiously: she is agitated. I stand sideways on the rope, wobbling slightly. Something isn't right. Plum may be dozing, but Lady is trying to tell me something.

Mercy follows my gaze. 'Can you hear anything?' I ask.

'Nothing. Maybe Lady doesn't like you walking the

rope,' she says. 'Keep going. You only have another ten steps or so.'

Lady always knows when something is wrong. I look down again. A soldier, head bowed to protect him from the branches, pushes through the bushes. He rides slowly towards the trees. He might not look up and see us, but he will see our horses and will surely notice the fire pit. He will know we are nearby, wait and then kill us.

Mercy's face is frozen in fear.

My legs start to shake.

Count.

100. 99. 98. 97.

I steady myself.

The soldier stops his horse next to Lady and Plum, his face still obscured by low-hanging branches. I drop the balancing branch down to distract him. He turns and leads his horse back to the trees until he is directly beneath the rope. I bend my knees, bounce on the rope and jump as high as I can. As my body falls, I grab the tightrope with both hands, swing my body backwards and then forward until my bare feet land in the soldier's back with the full force of the momentum. He falls awkwardly on his bottom and, releasing my hands from the rope, I land on my feet next to him.

The soldier looks up at me, his eyes green with a ring of gold around each pupil.

*

Elijah pulls himself up, dusts himself down and takes the reins of his oddly calm horse. 'You're lucky Arion is accustomed to conflict,' he says. 'And, I have to say, that's no way to greet me. You winded me badly! What on earth were you thinking?'

'You're a soldier?' I ask, putting my hand on my knife and backing slowly towards the shelter so that I can grab my sword. 'Why weren't you in uniform yesterday?'

'I wasn't supposed to be working,' he says, still catching his breath. 'But at the last minute the musketeers insisted I go with them to look for the Inseparables.'

'How did you know we were here?' says Mercy, still high up in the tree.

She slides down, grabs both swords from the shelter and hands me mine. I put mine back in its sheath, but Mercy keeps hers out, pointing it at the ground. She wants him to know that we are in control.

Elijah puts his hands up. 'I came here to talk, not fight.' He looks at me. 'I already knew that you're a decent sword fighter when you concentrate, Art, but I have to say that I'm astonished by your rope skills. And, as I said yesterday, I was impressed by the way you controlled your horse when she reared up yesterday.'

'And?' asks Mercy, her voice cold.

Elijah pretends not to hear her as he paces up and down. 'I don't know if Art told you, but I run the stables in the castle. So many of the boys go to war, but very few come back.'

He talks quickly, barely taking a breath. 'Art, you offered to help in the stables.' Mercy frowns at me and I silently mouth, *Later.* 'I don't know if you were serious, but the pay isn't bad and you would have free food and lodging. I can't pretend it's not hard work, particularly as the Witchfinder is unpredictable and likes to walk around the castle randomly quoting the Bible. Many times I've been hard at work when he has prodded me in the back and said, "The devil makes work for idle hands." But I don't think you are averse to the daily grind. What do you say? You would have to start today. This morning. Well, now. You would be doing me a favour that I would one day hope to repay.'

The amulet worked! I mustn't sound eager.

'Yes!' I say.

'Not so hasty!' says Mercy, grabbing my arm. 'Art and I work as a team and we need to discuss this. Privately. By the way, Elijah, you talk too much.'

'I do not!' Elijah says, but he leads his horse away until he is out of earshot.

'Let go of me,' I say to Mercy. 'Why do you hate him so much? This is what we – I – have been waiting for. A legitimate opportunity to go inside the castle. And now I have it. You can't stop me from going.'

'I'm not trying to *stop* you,' says Mercy. 'But you

cannot simply leave with a stranger. We need a plan.'

'I'm listening,' I say, looking over her shoulder to ensure Elijah has not already left.

'I understand that you are willing to risk your life to find your mother, but at least let me give you a selection of herbs and a poultice to protect you.' She glances at Elijah. His back is still turned, but she drops her voice so that I have to lean in to hear. 'Do not show them to *anyone* for people will, as well you know, brand you a witch. But first, give me your knife. It's sharper than mine.'

Mercy takes the knife and pulls me behind the fallen oak tree, so that we are completely hidden from Elijah. She turns her palm upwards and pushes the knife into her skin until it draws tiny droplets of blood. I stare, mesmerised. She wipes the knife on her trousers.

'Your turn,' she says, taking my arm and holding my wrist tightly. I expect my arm to shake, but it doesn't. Nor do I feel any pain as Mercy gently pushes the knife into my palm. When she holds up her palm, I do the same. We push our palms together so that our blood unites.

'Let us decree …' says Mercy solemnly.

I start to laugh; I know I am ruining the moment, but I cannot help it.

'Mercy. I mean, Mack. I am happy to be your blood sister. Or brother. But what's the plan? Elijah won't wait much longer.'

'I will give you the poultice and herbs now – oak bark, motherwort and snakeweed. Do you know about the last? It has a thick, black root that, when cut, is red. Its leaves are blueish green and its flowers are sometimes bright yellow, sometimes violet.'

Now is not the time to teach me this.

'I have already boiled the root and the leaves; the poultice will relieve a serpent's sting or an open wound. If you are hurt, God forbid, use snakeweed first and oak bark second. Drink motherwort to calm yourself. Do you have any questions?'

I shake my head.

'Most important of all,' she says, her voice catching. 'You must promise to come back to camp at dusk so we can discuss your plan of action.'

'I will be fine,' I say impatiently. 'I promise. I am fiercer and more determined than even I realised. If I feel weak, I will appear strong. Nothing bad can happen to me.'

'Good luck, dear Art,' she whispers.

I don't look at her in case I change my mind.

'I am ready, Elijah,' I say, mounting Lady. 'Take me to the castle.'

18

Elijah rides ahead, ignoring established pathways and instead pushing Arion through overgrown trees and bushes. The air is already thick with heat and flies bother the horses, forcing them to constantly twitch their ears and swing their tails back and forth like a pendulum.

Beads of sweat form on my upper lip where, were I a boy, tufts of hair would be appearing. My chest tightens as we get closer to the castle and I have to remember to breathe. In through my nose. *One. Two. Three.* Out through my mouth. *One. Two. Three. Four …*

Elijah turns to look at me. 'Why are you breathing strangely? Would you like to stop? Here, have some water,' he says, offering me his flask. He is so close that I can smell horses and hay and the delicate scent of rose water on him.

'I'm fine,' I say. 'Thank you. It's going to be a very hot day. Do you still think there will be a storm tomorrow?'

'I do. They say it will be the biggest storm for a long time, but that it will pass very quickly. At least it will clear the air.'

We reach the edge of the forest and the sun is so bright that I have to pull my cap right down. The castle sits in front of us, heat shimmering on the moat.

'We will go into the castle through the postern gate, which leads to the stables,' says Elijah. 'I have to give you something first.'

He rummages around in his pocket, pulls out a collection of small pebbles threaded together on a string and hands them to me.

'I made it myself,' he says proudly. 'I took the inner part of the bark of a large tree – an ash, I think – and boiled it until it turned into fibres. It had to be thin enough to thread fourteen small pebbles through it.'

'What is it?'

Elijah smiles. 'Have you never seen a necklace like this before? Fourteen pebbles with natural holes in them to ward off witches.'

I stiffen. Mercy was right. I shouldn't have come.

'The Witchfinder is a stickler for rules and rituals,' says Elijah. 'I'm not sure I believe in such things, but it's best to play along with his peculiarities. Put it around your neck and forget about it. You probably won't be asked to show it, but better to be shrewd.'

I hold on to Lady's saddle so that he can't see my shaking hands.

He's not sure he believes in 'such things'. In rituals or in witches? Don't ask him. Don't say a word. You are just a boy who forages in the woods, walks a rope and knows how to handle a horse. A boy who is as scared of witches as everyone else.

'Thank you,' I say, taking the necklace and putting it over my head, so it rests next to the amulet.

*

Elijah mutters, 'St John,' to the two guards at the postern gate and we are waved in to the castle. He has clearly underplayed his status in the castle or a simple password would never have sufficed – for all I know, he might even be the Witchfinder's right-hand man. As the gate is locked behind me, my stomach flips. Part of me wants to turn Lady around, demand the guards open the gate and let me canter all the way back to Kelso. The other part of me wants to dismount, fight the guards with my sword and rescue Mother. Here I am, finally in the castle, finally close to her. But I must wait. I must be patient.

The castle is crowded with people rushing around with baskets of food and fresh washing and armour. Beyond flint walls lie squares of earth overgrown with bright red berries and the soft pink of summer fruits. I have never seen such treasure. A wooden hut stuffed with hay is home to two dozen or more hens, some with entirely black plumage. I lead Lady across the courtyard, trying to look as though I belong. The stable buildings are dominated by a clock tower and an elaborate entrance arch. Horses doze in the back of the stables or hang their heads out in the sun, their eyes half-shut, ignoring the circling flies.

'You can tie Lady up there,' says Elijah, pointing at a shaded trough full of more oats and barley than I have seen in a lifetime. 'There's a horse that badly needs some exercise. He's in the stable right at the end. Yes, the black horse. A stallion called Obsidian.' I recognise him at once from the bridge. 'Can you take him into the paddock before it gets even hotter? He is easily unsettled, but I think you can handle him. The Witchfinder was supposed to be taking him out, but he has other things to attend to.'

Other things. Like preparing for the witch trials.

I nod. 'Yes, of course.'

*

The large paddock is empty. Obsidian is unpredictable and temperamental and unhappy to have a new rider. He tries to throw me to the ground when I mount him, canters around the paddock when I instruct him to walk and stops when I instruct him to trot.

I lean forward and whisper firmly in his ear. 'You *will* do as I say.'

His body is stiff, but I squeeze his flanks tightly and he transitions from a brisk trot to a canter and then a gallop and back to a smooth canter. As we ride around and around the paddock in circles, images flood my head. The attic in Kelso. Mother on the cart. Maude giving me the amulet. The endless trees pulling me in among them. The endless hunger. Mercy being suspended from the bridge as though she had no value at all. Elijah's unexpected grief for his father and mother. A future as yet unwritten.

Obsidian slows and then stops. Steam rises from his glossy coat. I press his flanks, but he ignores me.

'Come on, fellow,' I say. 'You need to warm down.'

Obsidian suddenly rears up so high and violently that

I slide off his back, managing to steady myself as I land on my feet. There has been no perceptible change in circumstance, nothing to make him lose his composure. The air is still, the sky is blue, the birds almost silent.

He stands in front of me, his ears pinned back, showing me the whites of his eyes. He is clearly distressed and the look in his eye unnerves me; he doesn't trust me at all.

'Did the stable boy break his leg while he was riding

you?' I ask gently. 'Has someone badly hurt you? I'd make you some motherwort tea if I thought you'd drink it.'

A crow hovers over the paddock, cawing loudly as it flies very close to Obsidian. Every horse I have ever known would bolt, but he doesn't move a muscle.

I look around, again and again, convinced I am being watched, but I can't see a soul.

I lead Obsidian back to his stable and bolt the door.

*

The other boys are busy grooming horses, their clothes covered in black and grey and copper hair, so I clean out the stable of the docile young grey horse adjacent to Obsidian.

My mind is racing.

How close is the dungeon? I am sure I can feel Mother's presence. Assuming she is still …

I squeeze the back of the horse's leg until she lifts her hoof and then clean it with a pick.

Dare I leave the stables and explore the grounds?

There is a thump on the stable next door. And another, louder this time. Is that Obsidian kicking the stable door? I carefully look out of the grey horse's stable. Several men are striding across the courtyard, preceded by a yapping dog. I retreat back inside and stand flat against the wall, behind the door.

They would have to actually come into the stable to see me. I have my sword. And my knife. But I am outnumbered.

My heart is banging like a hammer in my chest. The men stop outside Obsidian's stable. The stallion kicks the door again.

'What is this I hear about Obsidian being exercised too hard in the paddock?'

The voice is loud and pompous.

Everything he says is fabricated! My heart beats violently.

'Who did this to my beloved horse?' bellows the Witchfinder.

I close my eyes.

'We are not sure, sir,' one of the soldiers replies, a tremor in his voice. 'Elijah will know, sir. William and Matthew are looking for him. Sir.'

'I don't have time for this! I should be thinking about tomorrow's witch trials. Or, I should say, hangings. No one is interested in trials. They all confess in the end. Caesar! Stop barking or I will whip you too!'

Obsidian expected to be whipped; I should have guessed.

There is no talk or barking for a minute or two and I imagine the men walking back across the yard with a terrified dog. I relax my shoulders and take my hand off my sword just as someone slides the bolt on the grey horse's stable door.

I put my hand on my sword again.

Breathe in and out slowly and silently, through your nose.

223

I smell his breath before I see him, the stench of sulphur filling the stable.

Do not look behind the door. Do not look at me.

'How is my obedient filly doing today?' asks the Witchfinder.

He is unprotected. If I wanted to, I could kill him right now. And then his men would kill me.

The grey horse backs into the corner, showing the whites of her eyes.

'Sir!'

He turns around.

'We found Elijah, sir. He is waiting for you in your headquarters. Sir.'

The Witchfinder sighs and bolts the door behind him.

I tell myself that Elijah will say he was the one exercising Obsidian. I tell myself that Elijah won't say it was me because plucking a random foraging boy out of the forest to work in the stable just before solstice would get him into trouble. I have to believe he will protect me to protect himself.

When I dare to look out of the stable door, the yard is empty and iron grey clouds drift across the sun.

19

I have never used a whip on Lady before and I very rarely kick her, but now I dig into her flanks with my heels again and again, harder and harder.

'I don't want to hurt you, Lady. I'm sorry,' I say, gulping back sobs. 'So, so sorry. I was so close to Mother, but I made a mess of everything.'

I no longer care about the branches catching on my clothes or scratching my face. I ride deeper and deeper into the forest without thinking about where we are going. I want to be as far away from the castle and the smell of sulphur as I possibly can. I wish I was at the back of the church, sitting alone on the hard pew. I wish I was at home, missing Mother and talking to Malkin's ghost. I wish I was anywhere but here.

When we reach a burn, I dismount and let Lady dip her muzzle into the clear water. I crouch down, splash my face and watch light green dragonflies flitting forward and backwards, up and down, skimming the surface of the water.

I try to calm my mind and think logically. As far as I am aware, only Elijah and the postern gate guards knew I was in the castle; I left with a group of stable boys taking horses out to be exercised. If I'm lucky, no one will be pursuing me. Unless, of course, Elijah told the Witchfinder that it was me riding Obsidian.

Was I wrong to trust Elijah?

I am exhausted, but I force myself to stand up. I have one foot in one of Lady's stirrups when a tattered piece of paper nailed to a tree on the other side of the burn catches my eye. The water is deeper than it looks, but I don't notice. As I get closer to the paper, I see a drawing of three figures in flowing black cloaks with hoods obscuring their faces. *The Inseparables.* Above and below the drawing are two words written in faded black ink: *WANTED* and *REWARD.*

I rip it off the tree, tear it into tiny pieces and hang the pebble necklace Elijah gave me on the nail. 'I do not want to ward off witches, I want to welcome them.'

Rushing back to Lady, my sleeve catches on a shrub-like tree with small delicate flowers, blue-black fruit and dark, twisted branches. The blackthorn! One of Mother's most beloved plants. Other townspeople used the juice of the berries as a red dye or to make sloe gin, but Mother used it to clean infected blood and to strengthen a weak heart. She used the leaves to relieve a tickled throat and to bring hope to those who had all but lost it. The fat berries are sour as they burst in my mouth, but I swallow them greedily: I need a strong heart, and more than that, I need hope.

I take a handful, wrap them carefully in one of Mother's handkerchiefs and place it back inside my jacket pocket. When I have finished, my fingers are stained deep red.

*

The fox appears from nowhere, though she doesn't stop to smell the air or scratch her torn ear this time.

She looks at Lady and me with those intense eyes of hers, but how can it be the same fox?

I find myself following her, past the silver birch, the hazel and the aspen, its grey bark covered with lichen, its branches dripping with soft catkins like sleepy caterpillars. When Mrs Fox turns left at a crossroads, I turn left too.

And there, in front of me, is Mercy's camp.

*

'Art!' Mercy runs towards me, gasping. 'You are covered in blood! What happened?'

The scratches on my face certainly sting, but they are surely not that bad. I look at my stained hands and realise my face must be red too.

'The blackthorn,' I say.

I dismount as Mercy rummages around in her saddlebag, pulls out a square of old shirt and dips it in a pan of cooling water.

'I thought you were badly hurt,' she says, gently rubbing at the red juice stains on my hands. 'Or that you'd badly hurt someone. Here, wipe your mouth, but be careful of all those scratches on your face. I can't believe you left the castle physically unscathed and ended up back at camp looking as though you'd been in a fight. Come and sit by the fire.'

'Wait! Where did those horses come from?' I ask, pointing at the two dark grey horses and pale golden palomino tied up next to Plum.

My throat is dry. The soldiers followed me. They will take me away from Mercy.

I turn Lady around. *We must leave at once.*

Mercy takes one of my blood red hands. 'It's nothing to worry about, I promise. Tie Lady up and I will explain.'

Their weapons are neatly lined up. A musket. A sword. A wooden longbow and a quiver of arrows. They are facing away from me, but I know at once who they are. They sit with their backs straight, their legs crossed, their knees touching. Hoods obscure their faces.

I stand very still. 'Why are they *here*?'

'Sit down, Art. It is safe, I promise.' She turns to the

Inseparables. 'Take your hoods down.'

I stand opposite them and watch as, one by one, they carefully push their hoods back. They all have short, badly cut hair and pale faces. Two have brown hair, brown eyes and thin, angular faces. The third has straw-coloured hair, cornflower blue eyes and a fuller face. I am surprised by their ordinariness; I had expected them to look heroic in some way, but they look no different to Mercy or me, simply a few years older.

'This is my second cousin, Portia,' says Mercy, smiling proudly and pointing at a girl with the same piercing blue eyes as her. 'And this is Tam and Flo. They are twins.'

They each raise a hand and I awkwardly raise one of mine in response.

I sit down opposite the girls reluctantly, but keep my knees up in case I need to get to my feet quickly.

'Why didn't you tell me that you are related to the Inseparables?' I ask, trying not to sound disappointed.

'I wanted to tell you,' says Mercy. 'But I haven't seen them for well over a week – other than at a distance on the bridge, of course – and I truly didn't know if you would ever have the chance to meet them. I suppose I was worried that you might be captured by soldiers and questioned. I know you wouldn't give up any information easily or willingly, but it was simply one less thing to worry about. It's not because I don't trust you, Art.'

I pick at the skin on my fingers, but I don't say anything.

'The good news,' says Mercy triumphantly, 'is that they want to help you.'

'I hope you don't mind,' says Portia, pushing her hand through her hair. 'Mercy told us your story. I understand that you didn't expect us to be here. But there is no time to waste. The Witchfinder will hang all the women in his dungeon just before midnight tomorrow.' A shiver runs up my spine. 'He killed Tam and Flo's mother and ...' She looks at the fire, blinking furiously. 'His men killed my mother. We want justice.'

'We can help you find your mother,' adds Flo. 'Before it's too late.'

I look at Portia, Tam and Flo across the fire. They are willing to risk everything to avenge their mothers' deaths. Their mothers' *murders*.

'Thank you,' I say, so softly that the four girls have to lean close to the fire to hear. 'I am so sorry you lost your mothers and I am honoured that you want to help. But I am not sure I can return to the castle.'

I take a deep breath and tell them about the castle and Obsidian and hiding in the grey horse's stable. I tell them that the Witchfinder called Elijah to his quarters because he was concerned about Obsidian, but that I think I trust him not to betray me. I tell them about Elijah's father and then mother disappearing; I tell them that I am sure Elijah truly believes he wasn't loved and it makes him doubt himself. I tell them about the WANTED poster I tore down and, to explain my bloody hands to the Inseparables, gorging on the blackthorn berries that Mother loved. *Loves.* I don't mention the fox with the torn ear; I have no idea if she was real and I don't want them to ridicule me, or to treat me like a child.

Mercy puts another log on the fire. 'You say Elijah has had a difficult life, but we have all had difficult lives.' She takes Portia's hand and squeezes it tight. 'I am still not at all sure I trust him.'

I don't know if I do either. But I don't say anything.

'At the very least, Elijah knows about this camp,' says Mercy. 'I don't think it's safe to stay here long.'

'I understand why you are wary, Mercy, but I don't think Elijah would risk betraying Art,' says Portia. 'Or at least, not till morning. In which case he could still be useful, if only to allow her access to the castle.' She looks at me. 'We have a plan that we would like to share with you.'

Tam and Flo nod in unison.

'There are tunnels snaking beneath the castle, as you might expect,' Portia continues. 'Some are blocked with rubble, but others are clear – they are there, as I'm sure you know, to provide escape routes should the castle be attacked. One particular tunnel leads straight from a trapdoor in the stables – I think it's in the stable that belongs to one of the nervous horses the Witchfinder rides – to the bottom of the east wing. There it joins the old sewage tunnels and rises steeply all the way up to the turret directly opposite the Witchfinder's quarters in the west wing. As far as we can tell, steps have been carved into the sewage tunnels.'

'How do you know all this?' I ask.

Mercy puts her forefinger to her mouth and shakes her head at me.

'We found a very detailed map that we examined carefully,' says Tam. 'But sadly it was ruined in a downpour.'

'Why didn't you go in the tunnels yourselves?' I ask. 'You look like boys; surely you could have found jobs in the castle.'

'Of course, we were prepared to enter the tunnels ourselves, but it was clear we would never make it as far as the west turret,' says Flo.

'Because of the guards?' I ask.

Portia shakes her head. 'We know we could safely reach the turret of the east wing, but then there's no way any of us could access the west wing and many of the tunnels leading to it are blocked. It is less than five yards from one turret to the other, but it's four storeys high and there are iron spikes on the ground below.

'Mercy and I have a cousin, Aphra, who works in the kitchen, washing dishes and helping to prepare the food. She told us that the guards have their first ale of the day at around eleven o'clock. Mercy knows an excellent herbal remedy Aphra could put in the ale to knock them out for a good hour, perhaps even two. So we can deal with the guards …'

Mercy takes over. 'There are two doors to the dungeon,' she says, excitement rising in her voice. 'There are always guards at the main entrance, but there's a secret door very few know about, that can be accessed by the well. You probably noticed the well, next to the clock tower that leads to the stables. Anyway, the key to the secret door is in the Witchfinder's quarters.'

I nod, trying to remember the well, trying to take in all this new information.

'We thought you could take your rope in the tunnels, use it to cross from one turret to the other and take the key to the secret door.' Mercy smiles, triumphant.

My mind is spinning. 'And how would I attach the rope to the west turret?'

'At first we thought you could shoot the rope over with an arrow,' says Tam. 'But there is no time for me to teach you how to do that. It is a very useful skill; I can shoot twenty arrows in a minute. I can wound at two hundred and fifty yards and kill at a hundred yards.'

'Tam!' says Flo.

'Sorry,' says Tam. 'As I was saying, the Witchfinder's windows are always flung open in the summer. If you attach a weight – a rock, say – to one end of the rope, you should be able to throw it hard enough to reach the Witchfinder's window. You will have to ensure the rock catches on something at that end and you will then be able to pull the rope tight and tie it to the window frame in the east turret. Mercy tells us that you are incredible on the rope. We really think you can do it.'

I have never reached the end of the rope.

I hug my knees to my chin. 'And once I have found the key? Assuming the key is even there.'

'Make your way back along the rope,' says Mercy. 'Climb down the tunnels and then go straight down the well. As I said, very few people know about the secret door, so they wouldn't be suspicious.'

'Where will the Witchfinder be while I am trying to steal the key?' I ask.

'We are pretty sure that he will be gorging on a feast in the main hall,' says Flo. 'He insists on an early lunch most days. Aphra says he has napkins embroidered with the initials: "W.G." Decanters of deep red wine and flagons of amber ale. His French chef serves dishes that sound incredible: venison prepared three ways, a stewed calf's head, sparrows with cinnamon, tortoise stewed with eggs, nutmeg and sweet herbs. And that's just for lunch.'

'I don't think it sounds incredible,' I say quietly. 'It sounds greedy and gluttonous. Women are being sold as witches because people are so desperate to eat. It makes me sick to think of the Witchfinder gorging on all that food.'

'You are right,' says Flo, blushing. 'I don't know what I was thinking.'

'Everyone is tired and hungry,' says Mercy. 'I will warm up some potage for Art and the two of us will sleep.'

Mercy, Portia, Tam and Flo stand in a circle and hold hands. Mercy and Flo extend their hands to me. Flo squeezes my hand hard and I squeeze it back.

'These are for you,' says Portia, reaching into her coat pocket and handing me a bundle of tallow candles. 'To use in the tunnels.'

'Thank you,' I say. 'You are very kind.'

'We will meet again in the morning, once Art has had a chance to think about our plan,' Mercy says as her cousin and the twins mount their horses.

I smile gratefully at the Inseparables as they leave camp. Less than an hour ago, I didn't have a plan. And now I can think only of the well and the tunnels and the turret and my rope. I have never reached the end of the rope before, but this time I must do so. This time I will make it. I *must* make it.

20

21 June 1647

Summer solstice

The trees are covered in placards. WANTED. RANSOM. I try to rip them all off as we canter past, but Lady doesn't slow down. I seize one: a drawing of a girl with short hair. I look at it in disbelief: the girl is me. A man with a hood obscuring his face stands in a courtyard, holding up placards with numbers written on them. He discards them, one at a time. Eight. Seven. Six. Five. I have to stop him, I have to stop time itself, but I keep falling off the rope. I can't reach him. Four. Three. Two. I beg him to stop. One. Zero.

I awake drenched in sweat and look over at Mercy, who is still fast asleep. *At least I didn't shout this time.*

I creep out of the shelter and sip some cold motherwort, but it tastes vile and does little to calm me.

The sun is still low in the sky and the air is already oppressive. Perhaps Elijah was right about the storm coming today.

I go back inside the shelter to wake Mercy before I leave, but when I look down at her, with her clumsily cut hair, her leaf-covered blanket pulled right up to her chin, her mouth upturned in a vague smile, I can't bring myself to pull her out of her dream.

I tiptoe away from the shelter, put some of the oak bark poultice from Plum's saddlebags in my jacket pocket and untie Lady.

I take a stick and write in the soil by the fire:

TELL APHRA TO MAKE THE GUARDS SLEEP AT ONCE.

Lady's hooves thud on the hard, dry earth as she canters through the trees.

'Art! Stop!'

The voice behind me is familiar. I slow Lady down and turn around. The Inseparable pulls her black hood back just enough for me to see her face.

'Portia! What are you doing here?'

'I was about to ask you the same thing. I assume you are heading for the castle without Mercy?'

No time to waste making up excuses.

'Yes. I didn't …'

Portia holds up her hand. 'You don't have to explain. I will get word to Aphra that the guards are to be drugged.'

I have a sudden urge to dismount and hug Mercy's cousin, but I turn Lady back towards the castle and ride her across the hard earth once again.

*

The wind is like an invisible beast unleashed in the forest. It rips branches off young trees and makes their trunks shake. Rain pushes its way down through the dense canopy of trees and softens the hard ground.

The tempest stops as quickly as it started and suddenly the sky is blue and the sun hot. The fields smell sweet and fresh and a rainbow curves in front of the castle. I list its colours in my head. Red. Orange. Yellow. Green. Blue. Indigo. Violet.

We ride faster and faster across the fields, as though Lady is winged.

I can only hope the password won't have changed since yesterday; people gather herbs on Midsummer Eve and St John's Wort is thought to keep demons at bay and disempower witches.

I say, 'St John,' quickly when I reach the postern gate, my palms sweating, but the miserable guards, standing stiffly in their soaked uniforms, simply wave me in.

I ride Lady into the stable courtyard, through puddles

and past soaked bales of hay. Another drop of giant rain. A fierce gust of wind. The sun vanishes. Lightning breaks the sky in two. Now that I am no longer protected by trees, the rain is savage, attacking my exposed skin like a quiver of arrows.

The stable boys run for shelter, leaving horses rearing up in the courtyard. Taking advantage of the commotion, I guide Lady into an unused stable in the far corner of the yard, check that no one has seen us and put the tallow candles in my pocket, both coils of rope over my shoulder and hide the saddlebags behind the trough of water. I hold Lady's neck tightly, inhaling her smell, kissing her tenderly.

'This is not goodbye,' I whisper.

*

Obsidian is tied up outside his stable, rearing up in the rain.

I look around the yard. The stable boys are nowhere

to be seen. I go into Obsidian's empty stable and bolt it shut behind me. I try to avoid stepping in the piles of manure and kick the hay to the side of the stable. The rain is hammering so loudly on the roof that I fear it may cave in. No trapdoor. I take the shovel and move the manure. Still nothing.

And then I remember. Portia didn't name Obsidian. She just mentioned one of the Witchfinder's nervous horses.

My heart pounds.

I cannot check every single stable for a trapdoor.

I unlock Obsidian's door and move quickly into the docile young grey horse's stable next door. She looks up at me, a wary expression in her eyes, but then continues to doze in the corner – not even the storm seems to bother her. I push her gently to one side of the stable and kick away the hay. The trapdoor! The rain is no longer pummelling the roof and the yard is silent.

The stable boys will be returning to the yard any second.

I hide the shorter length of rope under some hay, bend down and clear the dust away from the trapdoor with my hands. I pull the metal ring, but the door doesn't budge.

The horse turns and stands at the door. She is, unknowingly, hiding me.

'Peter!' a boy shouts urgently right outside. 'I need a hand with Obsidian. He's out of control again!'

I take a deep breath and tug and tug and tug at the

metal ring. The door moves. I pull it with all my strength until there is enough space for me to squeeze into. The boy is still shouting for Peter's help as I stand on my tiptoes to light one of the tallow candles from high up on the stable wall and shine it down into the hole. A wooden ladder leads into darkness.

Thank you, moonstone.

I loop the rope around my waist, put one foot on the ladder and then the other. As I slide the trapdoor back into place, I'm sure I can hear Elijah's voice, but it quickly fades to nothing.

21

The candle flickers on the dusty walls inside the narrow tunnel. The ground is uneven beneath my feet and my clothes keep catching on the brick walls. Every now and then, when the tunnel curves towards the castle, I can stand up straight and stretch my aching back.

Rats' long, delicate tails whip from side to side, making a swishing noise against the walls, and dank water drips on to my head from the ceiling. I won't be distracted. I can't be.

When the tunnel reaches the castle, it tilts slightly upwards.

I walk, I crawl, I climb.

Aromas of rich meat drift from the kitchen and my stomach growls. I hear muffled voices and heavy footsteps, sometimes so close that I freeze.

I pull myself up through the tunnels.

Up and up.

Sweat trickles down my forehead, but there is no time to wipe it away.

When the tunnel briefly flattens out, I allow myself to stop and catch my breath. Without warning, large lumps of masonry fall from the slope ahead and instinctively I move backwards, shielding my face, but still my mouth is dry and chalky with dust. I spit on the floor and wipe the fine dust from my eyelashes.

The candle has gone out.

Think quickly. Think. I cannot stay here. I cannot go back. There is no other way through.

I have an idea! I push a large lump of rock into my pocket and push at the floorboards above me, working my way from left to right and moving backwards down the tunnel. Finally, one moves. I lift it up, peer through the narrow gap and blink at the bright light. No sign of any guards. The floorboard is just wide enough to squeeze through. I push myself up.

Guards' voices, moving closer. I kick the floorboard back into place and quickly stamp on it so that it is secure. I look left and right: too dangerous. Just down the corridor is an open window. Boots march loudly along the corridor towards me.

I push the window wide open, hold on to the frame and pull myself up. There is a sharp drop below; I am already near the top of the castle.

Don't look down. Never look down.

The voices are moving closer.

Remember to breathe.

The ledge is wider than I had dared hope. I put my back against the wall.

It's all about balance.

The two guards stop near the window.

'Do you think we will be given his leftovers today?' asks one.

'Probably not,' says the other. 'He's far too mean. I'm

ravenous, but I'm still not sure I fancy stewed tortoise. Perhaps we can make do with this ale while we're guarding the east turret.'

They laugh.

Did Portia get the message to Aphra quickly enough? Did she put the herbs in their ale?

'I'll shut this window first, in case the heavy rain returns.'

He pulls the window to and their footsteps recede.

I inch back towards the window and push at it with both my shaking hands, but it doesn't give. I thrust my hips forward with all my might. The window flies open and I tumble on to the floor, curling myself into a ball to land as quietly as possible.

Using my knife, I quickly find the loose floorboard. I light another of my tallow candles from a candle on the wall and lower myself back down into the tunnel.

*

As the tunnel snakes upwards, it is wider and taller than before.

This is going to be more straightforward. I can make up for lost time.

When the tunnel flattens out, I notice the floor is scattered with fragments of pale shell. I bend down to pick a piece up. It's hard and smooth and, upon closer inspection, slightly yellow. I toss it back on the floor.

The tunnel twists to the right. The candle quivers. I hold it up.

I blink hard.

And look again.

Ahead is a dense wall of unbroken yellow shells, all of a similar size.

My breathing becomes erratic, as though the air has thinned out. I stagger backwards, stifling a scream.

They are not shells. They are skulls. *A wall of trophies.*

I walk slowly towards the wall, moving the candle

up and down, from left to right.

The skulls are packed tightly together and each is branded with the same letter.

W.

I walk towards the wall as if in a trance.

I kick the bottom layer with all my might and watch as the wall of skulls collapse.

'This is where it ends,' I say, not even bothering to whisper. 'Hopkins will kill no more.'

*

When I reach the end of the tunnel and push myself carefully up through a few loose floorboards, I see the two guards lying slumped against a wall, snoring gently, the empty flagon of ale tipped on to its side.

Thank you, Aphra! Thank you, Mercy and Portia and the twins.

I carefully remove the key chain from the first guard's belt, holding my breath to avoid the stink of stale ale oozing from his motionless body. There are a dozen keys on the chain, but the keyhole to the turret door is unusually large and I quickly find the right one.

The door makes a terrible squeak. I stand still for a moment as one guard rolls in his sleep and the other suddenly stops snoring, as if he has been disturbed, but neither opens his eyes.

I lock myself inside the turret and lean against the door, waiting for my heart to steady itself.

Tie the rope around the rock. Throw the rope into the west turret window. Walk the rope. Find the key. But … what if the Witchfinder is in his quarters, waiting for me? What if Elijah told him that I was the one who exercised Obsidian?

I look around the room, my heart still beating fast. It is sparsely furnished: a bed, a wardrobe, a chair and a heavy wooden desk in front of the window.

I remove my sword from its sheath and place it carefully under the bed. As I stand back up, I see a shape out of the corner of my eye. A ghost with brutally short hair. I stifle a laugh as I move closer to the wardrobe. Of course Hopkins is vain enough to have huge, expensive mirrors in his castle; he even named his horse after the dull, unpolished stone. I gingerly touch the mirror and stare at myself, covered from head to toe in white dust from the tunnel.

I quickly brush myself down, tie the rock to the end of the rope and focus on the turret directly opposite the window where I am standing. The Witchfinder's windows are flung wide open. I kiss the moonstone in relief.

Taking a deep breath, I throw the rope towards the west turret. It falls short and I quickly reel it back in. I take a step backwards, aim the rock carefully and throw it with all my might. Unbelievably, it lands in the Witchfinder's room. I move the rope around until the stone catches on the corner of the window frame, then tie my end of the rope tightly on the stone mullion dividing the windows in two.

I kick off my boots and place my cap next to them.

After the storm, the sky is a perfect blue, the cirrus clouds mere wisps of white.

I glance down at the courtyard thronged with guards and soldiers, servants carrying piles of food to and from the kitchen. Everyone is much too busy to even think of looking up.

I can just about make out the clock tower in the stables. Forty minutes past eleven.

The moonstone burns against my chest. It is now or never.

The rope is taut, with a slight dip in the middle. I wish I had a branch to help me balance, but the sheath will have to do. I hold it firmly and stand tall. I swallow and take a deep breath.

One. Two.

The rope is rough beneath my feet.

I am thankful that the wind has dropped. There is

barely even a breeze.

Three. Four.

With each step, I take another deep breath.

Five. Six.

Swallows dip and swoop around me, as though comforting and encouraging me.

Seven. Eight. Nine. Ten.

I am halfway.

A ladybird alights on my hand. 'Ladybirds bring luck,' Mother used to say. 'Try not to kill one, even by accident, for it will bring sadness and misfortune.'

I stand perfectly still.

I am scared.

I am brave.

I am strong.

I am alive.

I am, I am, I am.

The ladybird lifts its gossamer wings and flies away.

I walk as if in a trance.

Eighteen. Nineteen.

My feet quiver on the rope. *Don't lose focus now.* I take three slow, deliberate breaths and stagger forward to catch the window frame.

I completed my first walk!

For a brief, blissful moment, I forget where I am.

22

The candle throws shadows across the small, empty room. A heavy wooden desk is covered in paper, an extravagant chaise longue is covered in silk and two lavishly upholstered armchairs and a small table face the fireplace. The local newspaper is folded up on one of the armchairs. I glance at the headline:

ELIZABETH CLARKE HAS SUCKLED IMPS

I throw it on to the fading fire, which roars back into life. I curse myself for being impulsive and potentially drawing attention to myself.

I must be quick. The desk drawers are, to my surprise, unlocked. And every single one is empty. I look around frantically.

The key has to be in here.

There are footsteps – and voices – down the corridor.

A large square mirror sits on the mantelpiece above the fire. I tilt it forward and run my hand down the back. Something cold, metallic. The key! I put it safely inside my pocket.

I tie the rope securely to the stone mullion. As I stand up, I notice a flash of silver on the small table.

My skin prickles.

Dread creeps through my body, like black ink.

A white moonstone flecked in blue is attached to the silver chain. Mother's necklace. She said that one day it would be mine, but not like this. I put it around my neck and tuck it beneath my shirt, so that it hangs beside the moonstone Maude gave me.

'Mother, meet Maude,' I whisper as I step back out on the rope. 'Maude, meet Mother.'

*

The rope cuts the soles of my feet, but I barely notice.

I can think only of Mother.

I always felt in my heart that she was in the castle, but now I *know* she is here.

I put one bloodied foot in front of the other, counting carefully, balancing easily, breathing evenly.

*

The room in the east turret is exactly as I left it, yet it is as though everything has somehow transformed in the brief time I have been gone. The sun colours the room an intense orange and I step into the light with new purpose.

I quickly untie the rope and let it drop silently beneath the Witchfinder's window. The clock tower chimes twelve times. I pull my boots back on, slip my cap on, reattach my sheath to my belt and slide my sword from under the bed.

The guards are snoring outside the door, the flagon of ale still on its side. I lock the east turret door and find a gap in the floorboards to drop the key into.

I walk quickly, quietly, until I reach the window I had to push open not so long ago. I force open the same floorboard with my knife, praying no more masonry has fallen.

'The key to the east turret!' shouts one of the guards groggily in the distance.

Maybe I should have risked returning it to his ring of keys.

I light another candle from the candle on the wall and lower myself into the tunnel.

'You lost it! Don't blame me …'

'The door is locked!'

I hear them forcing the door with all their weight.

I pull the floorboard back into place and move swiftly back down the tunnel.

*

I replace the trapdoor in the docile grey horse's stable, find the second coil of rope and tie it around my waist. I stand for a moment and listen. The stable boys are mucking out the stables, grooming the horses, talking about the storm and wondering when their next meal might be.

I dust down my clothes as best I can and wipe my face on my shirt, trying not to focus on the exhaustion creeping into every corner of my body.

I step out of the stable and stride straight towards the well, past people weaving from left to right and shouting instructions at each other. They clutch boxes of fish and baskets laden with freshly picked vegetables and do their best to avoid the puddles.

I look around, hoping that no one will notice me. There's the kitchen, with rabbits hanging by the door. To the left, two stout guards in front of a heavy wooden door with half a dozen bolts across it. If that is the main door to the dungeon, Portia and the twins were right: I will never get past them.

I step to the left to peer through an arch in the brick wall.

Look away.

Men are tying lengths of rope to poles.

Look away right now.

The ropes are blowing in the breeze. My stomach lurches.

Nausea is replaced with a surge of raw, pure fury. I put my rope over my shoulder and start to pull at the grille covering the well.

Huge drops of rain start to fall.

A man runs out of the kitchen, his apron bloody.

'The kitchen is going to flood!'

I pull at the grille. It barely moves. It is much too heavy for me to move on my own.

The cook pushes his way past panicked gardeners and bakers and blacksmiths until he reaches the well.

'I have been instructed to descend into the well to open the gates to the cellars, to release the rain water into the moat,' I shout above the din.

We stand side by side and pull.

A soldier in uniform stops by the well.

'We have to open the cellar gates,' says the cook.

The soldier peers into the well. 'You had better hurry up. It's filling with water.'

When the grille is halfway across the well, I thank the cook. I can do the rest on my own.

*

I am about to tie the rope to the arch stone when someone puts their hand on my shoulder.

I freeze.

'The girls want you to know that they are all here for you. As am I, should you need me.'

I turn around.

'Elijah?'

'I am he. Pretend I am helping you tie the rope.'

We thread the rope through the arch stone and tie a firm knot.

'I know everything,' he says. 'About you and Mercy and her cousin and the twins.'

'I don't know what you are talking about,' I say casually, as I drop the rope down the well.

'I came to your shelter this morning because I didn't know what else to do. Mercy told me everything.'

Elijah lowers his voice. 'When the Witchfinder called me to his quarters in the west turret to find out who had been exercising Obsidian, I naturally told him it was me. He has never been a kind man, but now I see him for who he is: he would be King of Essex, if not England, but he is no more than a beast. My aunt forced me to work here and send money to her. I have always kept my head down and done what I am told.'

'I don't understand the point of this story,' I say, looking down the well and watching the water slowly rise.

'I will be quick. I saw the Witchfinder kick Caesar as I was walking into his quarters. The poor dog was cowering behind an armchair, shivering. The Witchfinder started to boast about the midsummer hangings and his face was twisted with hate in the firelight.'

'He isn't king of anything,' I say, 'but rather the Prince of Darkness.'

'He is also very powerful, so you need to be quick. The guards in the east turret will be awake by now.'

I climb on to the circular wall, hold the rope tight and start to lower myself down the well.

'By the way,' says Eljah, 'I know you are a girl. It

makes no difference to me. Good luck.'

He squeezes my shoulder before I descend into darkness again.

23

100. 99. 98. 97. 96.

The wall is slimy and slippery.

95. 94. 93. 92.

The rope is tied tightly to the stone arch. It will not break.

91. 90. 89.

I can't see anything.

88. 87.

I gently bounce off the walls.

86. 85.

Rain pours down.

84.

What if I can't access the door?

83.

What if the Witchfinder already killed Mother and took the moonstone as a trophy?

82. 81. 80. 79. 78. 77. 76.

Breathe.

75. 74. 73.

I feel for the key. Still in my pocket.

72. 71.

'Who goes there?'

The voice echoes down the well. I stay silent.

The rope quivers.

70. 69. 68. 67.

'Pass me a knife!'

66.

I am nearly at the bottom. A soldier cuts the rope

and I fall.

*

There is a splash as my body hits the water at the bottom of the well, but I hope the soldier doesn't hear. If he knows there was a body attached to the rope, he will be alerting everyone, including the Witchfinder.

My shoulders ache and my ankle is badly cut, but I don't have long. I take the oak bark from my pocket, slip it inside my boot and press it gently against my ankle. I take the key and touch the walls until I find the secret door. I feel for the keyhole, put the key in and turn it triumphantly. It doesn't move.

The water is up to my knees.

It must be the wrong key.

I wriggle it from left to right, from right to left, but it doesn't give. I turn the key more gently and it works. The door creaks open and the water floods out from the well. The stink is foul; not of death, but of the anticipation of

279

near death. Low, persistent wailing echoes off the walls.

My ankle is hot with pain, but I ignore it. I tiptoe forward, my hand on my sword.

I look for a set of keys to open the cells. I find it easily, hanging from a rusty hook.

I shiver; the air is damp and holds a wintry chill. The first three cells on both sides of the corridor are empty. I take a step closer to the fourth cell on the left.

I am in one of my own nightmares.

There are perhaps thirteen women in a tiny space, their ankles in iron gauntlets, arms stretched upwards, fastened to the walls at the wrist. Their thin bodies, clothed in filthy rags, hang limply. One of the women, her hair tangled, looks up and mouths something at me.

I don't know what she's saying.

I look again.

'Help me.'

I cannot help anyone until I have found Mother.

*

There is a dull thump of thunder above; the storm has returned.

I walk slowly down the corridor, looking at the women in the flickering candlelight.

The dull thump is closer. It isn't thunder, but gunshot.

I realise far too late that I cannot get out of here. The rope to get back out of the well has been cut and the main door is bolted and protected by guards.

I walk more quickly.

'Mother?'

I look into each cell.

I am nearly at the end of the corridor.

'I have your moonstone, Mother.'

The doors to the dungeon burst open.

'Found him!' A guard runs at me, dagger in one hand, sword in the other. I nimbly sidestep him. He turns, his enraged face made ghostly by the candlelight, his weapons raised. I thrust my sword forward, jabbing him in the stomach. At an angle, upwards, towards the heart. He drops his dagger.

A large hand circles my neck. One guard in front of me, albeit injured, and another behind.

Think quickly.

I turn slightly and firmly raise a knee to the second guard's groin. He releases his grip around my neck.

The first guard, his shirt stained crimson, lunges towards me. I dance to the side. As he falls to the ground, he stabs the second guard in the upper leg. The second guard lurches forward, crying out, the weight of his weapon tilting towards my right arm. His sword tears my shirt and grazes my skin.

The second guard tries to stem the flow of blood on his leg.

'Help me,' he says.

I pay no attention to him.

Every nerve in my body is tingling.

I run back up the corridor, my ankle miraculously healed.

'Agnes!'

I strain my ears.

'Art?'

'Mother?'

My head is spinning. I feel sick and tired and wide awake and scared and ...

'Art, is that really you?'

I cry out with joy. I had almost forgotten the soft, reassuring sound of Mother's voice. Tears run down my cheek.

Her cell is dark. I take a candle from the corridor and push a key into the lock. It doesn't fit. I try the second. It fits. My hand is shaking. I turn it and push open the door.

I lift the candle up. I can't see anyone.

Not a ghost. Not a ghost. Please, not a ghost.

'I am here, Art.'

Sitting in the corner, her wrists and ankles are shackled, her beautiful red hair hacked short. Her cheeks hollow, her skin as pale as the moon. But, nonetheless, she is my mother.

I put the candle down, take a key for the shackles from a hook and pull her carefully to her feet. I put my left arm around her waist, smelling the faintest scent of lavender and woodsmoke.

I reach inside my jacket pocket and take out the bloodied handkerchief. 'These are for you, Mother.'

'Blackthorn, for a strong heart and hope.' She eats the squashed berries greedily. 'You remembered, Art. You remembered.'

*

I help Mother up the stairs, getting ever closer to the clash of metal, of grunts, shouts and wails of pain. I hold my sword with my right hand, expecting more guards to come running down the stairs, brandishing their swords and knives.

None come.

The dungeon doors are wide open. Mother blinks furiously.

Men and women stream out of the kitchen, running back through the puddles with loaves of bread and baskets of wood. They run through the postern gate and disappear. I count four, no, five soldiers. And, at a glance, four more on horseback. I look again. Three of those on horseback wear black capes, their hoods up. The fourth wears a cap pulled tightly down.

They came!

I find a wooden stool, a plate of bread and cheese and a discarded bottle of ale.

'Sit here, Mother,' I say. 'Eat this food if you can. I will come back for you and we will free the other women, I promise.'

She simply nods, her body slumped forward with weakness.

I kiss her head and run into the courtyard. Mercy, Portia and the twins have dismounted and Elijah is holding the reins of all four horses, leading them hurriedly to the stables, a look of great purpose on his face.

Mercy is fighting an overweight guard. She parries, lunges and nicks him on the soft side of his wrist. To her right, Portia shifts her weight from one leg to another, moving back and forth with her sword and outwitting a tall, wiry guard.

I look up. A soldier runs towards me with a knife.

He is strong. I must be stronger.

I take my sword out and knock the knife from his hand. He walks backwards, both hands raised. Another soldier comes at me with a sword. I extend my right leg and propel my body forward with my back leg. Swords clash.

I lunge forward, backwards, forward. He catches my

right arm and the sword breaks my skin, drawing blood. The pain is searing, but I ignore it. I advance with such force that I knock his sword out of his hand and watch, in horror, as my own sword flies through the air and clatters to the ground.

A dog barks.

I turn towards the castle. Caesar is standing in the doorway of the kitchen.

I look at Flo pointing her musket at two soldiers.

Tam has an arrow in her longbow, which I notice now is made of the smoothest pale yellow yew.

The dog suddenly stops barking and lies on the ground, whimpering.

The Witchfinder fills the doorway, his red cape billowing in the wind. He steps out of the doorway, his expression of disgust almost comical, a jewel-encrusted dagger in his hand.

Flo points her musket at him.

Tam pulls her arrow back.

She said she can wound at 250 yards and kill at 100 yards. She is less, much less, than 100 yards away from him. I hope she wasn't boasting for no reason.

An arrow soars through the air. I watch it, open-mouthed. Hopkins drops his dagger. He stands there for a second, the arrow driven deep into his eyeball. There is a look of utter astonishment on his face. And then he falls backwards on to the hard, cold kitchen floor. Caesar jumps up and licks his face.

Tam takes a step forward, as though thinking of reclaiming the arrow.

'Leave it,' I say, putting a hand on her arm.

'Rest in peace,' mutter his soldiers without much compassion, as they limp towards the postern gate.

Mercy stares at the Witchfinder and his deserting soldiers in disbelief and then steps over the overweight guard lying very still at her feet to stand next to me.

'Please,' I say. 'Tell all the women in the dungeon that it is safe to leave.'

'Yes, of course. Portia and the twins can do that. You should sit down for a moment, Art, you look terribly tired.' She turns to face me and puts both her hands on my shoulders. 'But you did it. You actually did it! I shall never forget your determination to find your mother.'

'Horses,' is all I manage to say in response. 'Mother and I need horses. Please.'

She nods.

I turn to the doorway of the dungeon and see Mother wiping crumbs from her mouth.

'Mother!'

I run to her as fast as I can, in case she vanishes again. I take her in my arms and hold her thin body tight and whisper, 'I love you, I love you, I love you.'

She holds me close and then pushes me gently away to look at me, as though I might be a ghost.

'Your face is very white, as though you've spent the day baking cakes. And, Art, your hands are bloody!' she exclaims, as if bloodied hands are something I should be worried about after everything I have been through to get here.

'It's just chalk dust from the tunnels and juice from the blackthorn. You know how badly it stains,' I say, laughing. Then I see that a little blood is running down my right arm so I take the oak bark from inside my boot and hold it against the cut.

Mother smiles. 'I see you have been using my recipe book.'

'Yes,' I say. 'And my friend Mercy knows a thing or two about herbal remedies.'

The world starts spinning slightly too fast and I hold on to the wall for a moment to steady myself.

'You will be strong again soon,' says Mother, softly stroking the dried tears on my cheeks.

'I am strong now, Mother, because of the moonstone. In fact, because of *both* moonstones.' I reach inside my shirt to show Mother the necklace that Maude gave me, but it has gone and only Mother's moonstone remains.

She shakes her head. 'You are strong because of *you*.' Her voice is hoarse, but I know she won't cry. 'I knew that if you were ready to make the journey, you would find me.'

'I was open to the guides I met along the way, Mother,' I say. 'Just as you told me. But I couldn't have done this without my new friends.' My voice is unsteady and I don't want to cry again, so I turn to look at Mercy and Elijah leading Plum and Lady towards us.

'May I?' asks Mercy and I nod. She walks slowly to Mother, her head slightly bowed as if she is shy, and then suddenly she is embracing Mother, her head buried on Mother's shoulder.

Finally, when Mercy has pulled away, Mother takes

her hand between both of hers. 'Thank you for guiding my daughter.'

'I think *she* guided *me* ...' says Mercy, smiling. She hands Plum's reins to Mother. 'Please take my horse. She is scared by nothing and no one. I can take the docile grey when I leave.'

I try to argue, but Mercy holds her hand up to stop me. 'You will always remember me if you have Plum.'

The Inseparables, their hoods down, turn and lift their hands to say goodbye before starting their descent into the dungeon.

'Thank you,' I say to them. 'For everything.'

I stare hard into the doorway, but it's as though they were never really there.

'Where will you go?' asks Elijah.

'We cannot go back to Kelso,' I say. 'Not for a long time.'

'I was thinking of the west coast of Scotland,' says Mother. 'Perhaps we can go to one of the islands where no one will care about herbal remedies and old wives' tales.'

'I like the sound of that,' I say, helping her on to Plum.

I look at Mercy and Elijah.

Mercy holds out her arms. I hug her tight. I never want to let her go. I turn to Elijah and embrace him too. He smells of horses and hay and rose water.

'Goodbye, sweet Art,' he says, the golden rings in his eyes glittering in the sun.

'Goodbye, dear friend,' says Mercy. 'Think of me sometimes.'

'I shall think of you always,' I say, mounting Lady.

We don't look back. We must go forward now, forever forward.

*

We ride north, my mother and I, away from the castle of death. Finally, we stop at the edge of a forest so that Mother can catch her breath.

As we turn back towards the trees, a fox with a torn ear trots past, followed closely by her cubs.

Acknowledgements

Unceasing thanks to ...

Carol Raphael for instilling the importance of reading in me at a very young age (not sure why I tried to read Solzhenitsyn at seven, but I was never told I couldn't) and, equally importantly, for checking everything equine in this book.

Bonnie Raphael Irvine for reading endless drafts and freely offering up her sometimes brutal teenage wisdom.

Sarah Strickland, Jon Wilde, Fiona Macintosh, Lizzie Frankie, and Clare Drysdale for reading various versions and giving great notes.

Becky Thomas for persevering and pulling off a two-book deal with such an excellent publishing house. Your indefatigable support paid off ...

Polly Lyall Grant for believing in this story the moment she read

it, for invaluable ideas on how to improve the book, for sharing a love of cats and witches and feminist folklore fables.

Steve Coogan for being passionate about the initial idea, for making me laugh and for giving me a place to write.

Becca Langton for some crucial early notes.

Kate Mosse for the 'keep going' advice that every writer needs (ideally on a daily basis, but really any time will do, especially if coffee is involved).

Parisa Taghizadeh for taking my author pic in exchange for an oxygen-giving plant.

Corina Buckwell for providing the best place in England to write and for long chats about children's books.

Paul Vincent for keeping me in the moment with Qi Gong, a skill I hopefully passed on to Art Flynt.

August Ro for the gorgeous front cover and meticulous inside illustrations. Спасибо!

Everyone at Hachette Children's Group who supported (and continue to support) the book in the most glorious ways imaginable:

Katherine Agar, Dominic Kingston, Emily Finn, Alice Duggan, Katherine Fox, Annabel El-Karim. Thank you also to Jenny Glencross.

Finally, I learned all about herbs and their medicinal uses via The Complete Herbal, *Nicholas Culpeper's seminal book from the early 1600s, now available online as a free e-book. Meanwhile, these history books helped to educate me about the English Civil War and the brutal murder of hundreds of so-called witches:* The English Civil War at First Hand *by Tristram Hunt;* Witches *by Tracy Borman and* Witchfinders *by Malcolm Gaskill.*

P.S. 'Evil witches' are just powerful women.

AMY RAPHAEL has been writing about popular culture and sport for three decades. As a journalist, Amy has freelanced for all the UK broadsheets as well as magazines such as Elle and Rolling Stone, interviewing over a thousand icons along the way. She has written half a dozen non-fiction books, including Danny Boyle: Creating Wonder and A Seat at the Table: Women on the Frontline of Music. This is her first children's book. She lives in Hove with her daughter and their cat.

AUGUST RO is an illustrator from a small town in the Far East. Inventing stories and telling them in her illustrations is what she truly loves. Her dream is to live in the forest and make friends with deer!